This is a tale about a dog we called Savage
Sam. It's partly about me, too, and about
Papa and Little Arliss and a girl named
Lisbeth Searcy and some others. But it's
mainly about Sam, on account of without
him, there wouldn't have been much of a
tale to tell or anybody left to tell it.

Papa was the one named him Savage Sam.
He did it as a joke. This was back when
Sam was still just an old clumsy big-footed,
rump-sprung pup, sort of liver-speckled,
with flop-hound ears, a stub tail and a
pot belly that was all appetite....

SAVAGE SAM was originally
published by Harper & Row.

# SAVAGE
# SAM

by Fred Gipson

PUBLISHED BY POCKET BOOKS NEW YORK

SAVAGE SAM

Harper & Row edition published February, 1962

*Pocket Book* edition published June, 1963
7th printing......September, 1970

This *Pocket Book* edition includes every word
contained in the original, higher-priced edition. It is printed
from brand-new plates made from completely reset, clear, easy-to-read
type. *Pocket Book* editions are published by Pocket Books, a division
of Simon & Schuster, Inc., 630 Fifth Avenue, New York, N.Y. 10020.
Trademarks registered in the United States and other countries.

L

Standard Book Number: 671-55082-9.
Library of Congress Catalog Card Number: 62-7948.
*Printed in the U.S.A.*

*This book I dedicate to some mighty loyal and faithful companions—every hogdog, cowdog, trailhound and flea-infested kitchen-robbing potlicker mongrel who helped to make a Big Adventure of my childhood.*

—FRED GIPSON
*Mason, Texas*

# SAVAGE
# SAM

*Sam*

*One*

THIS is a tale about a dog we called Savage Sam.
It's partly about me, too, and about Papa and Little Arliss and a girl named Lisbeth Searcy and some others. But it's mainly about Sam, on account of without him, there wouldn't have been much of a tale or anybody left to tell it.

Sam's papa was Old Yeller, known as the best catch dog and the worst camp robber in all our part of the Texas hill country. His mama was a blue-tick trail hound belonging to Lisbeth's grandpa, Bud Searcy, a blowhard neighbor of ours who lived over in the Salt Licks settlement.

Sam was born in a badger hole and given to us by Lisbeth.

Papa was the one who named him Savage Sam. He did it as a joke. This was back when Sam was still just an old clumsy, big-footed, rump-sprung pup, sort of liver-speckled, with flop-hound ears, a stub tail and a pot belly that was all appetite.

I remember when Papa did it. Mama had set a panful of table scraps out in the yard for Sam. Greedy as always,

Sam was gulping those scraps down like he couldn't wait. Papa stood watching him. Finally, his eyes started twinkling and he went to pulling at one horn of his long black mustache.

"It appears to me," he said, speaking extra sober, "that when it comes to tackling a wheat-flour biscuit or a chunk of roast venison, we own about the most savage dog in the State of Texas!"

This set us all to laughing; and after that, we started calling him "Savage Sam."

As it turned out, the name wasn't a bad fit. For Sam would fight. Even as a pup, he'd fight. He had that much of Old Yeller in him.

You couldn't count all the battles he used to pull off with the passel of house cats that always followed Little Arliss to the cowpen at milking time.

Little Arliss was my brother. He was about six then, and just learning to milk. He wasn't doing a bad job of it, either, except that he got so little milk in the bucket. Most of it he squirted into the open mouths of the mewing cats. It tickled him to angle the milk streams so high above their heads that the cats had to rear up on their hind legs and prance around, trying to catch it.

Then here would come Sam, wanting his share of the milk. This always made the cats mad. They'd jump on him, clawing and squawling. And while Sam couldn't whip them yet, still, he had the grit to stand his ground and make a fight of it.

I'd hear the commotion and come running, yelling at Arliss to quit fooling with them cats and get the milking done. Arliss, he'd yell back, telling me to shut my mouth and let him alone. And when I didn't, he was just as liable as not to pitch his milk bucket into the cowpen dirt and grab up a rock to throw at me.

Being about fifteen at the time and considered too big to fight back, I'd have to skin out for the house, hollering for help. Then here would come Mama, calling for Arliss to behave himself before she took a mesquite sprout to him. Behind her would come Papa, ready to back up her threat, if need be, but always laughing his head off at the general all-round hullabaloo.

2

Well, anyhow, Sam still wasn't much more than a big overgrown pup, maybe eighteen months old, when this bad trouble hit us.

It was in the first days of September in 1870 or '71; I disremember which.

I do recollect that me and Papa had just finished grubbing brush off a patch of new ground we planned to break and sow to winter wheat. It was nearly dinnertime. We shouldered our grubbing tools and packed them off to the cabin.

We were hot and thirsty and tired. We drank half the water in the brassbound cedar bucket hanging by a chain from a pole rafter in the dog run. We sat down in cowhide-bottomed chairs and leaned back against the walls. We let the south breeze blow against our sweaty clothes, drying them out and cooling us off. We yanked out the spines of prickly pear and tasajillo cactus that had our britches pinned to our legs.

Mama came out to sit with us while she churned a batch of sour cream, hoping to get fresh butter by the time the cornbread browned for dinner.

We'd all just got good settled when we heard a sound that jerked us to our feet. It was the clatter of horse hoofs coming at a dead run along the trail that led beside Birdsong Creek.

We stepped out into the clear. We shaded our eyes with our hands to break the blinding glare of the sunlight, and looked down the slope toward the spring where we got our drinking water.

Giant live oaks, cottonwoods, and bur oaks grew beside the spring. Mustang-grape vines drooped from their branches. Trees and vines laid down such a black shade that it was hard to see anything under them. Then I caught a flash of movement and Papa said, "Why, it's old Blowhard Bud, himself! Wonder what sort of bur he's got under his tail this time."

We stood and waited till Bud Searcy came galloping out of the shade, spurring his crowbait horse into a final sprint up the slant toward our cabin. Riding behind him, holding to the cantle of the saddle, was Lisbeth.

The second they rode into the sunlight, I knew something was wrong. I could tell by the long-barreled shotgun Searcy packed across his saddle bow. I could tell by the six-shooter and bowie knife that hung from a leather belt he wore around his fat belly. Mostly, I could tell by the way Searcy rode, with his head held high and jerking from one side to the other like an old steer scenting blood.

Then he was sliding his jaded horse to a stop at our frontyard gate and fixing us all with a wild, fierce stare.

*"Injuns!"* he shouted. "Raiding all over the country!"

Mama gasped. I felt a little cold snake of fear go wiggling along my backbone and noticed how Papa suddenly stiffened.

"Indians?" Papa said. "Where? At Salt Licks?"

"No," Searcy said. "At Loyal Valley. Run off a bunch of horses there last night!" He turned to Lisbeth and said in a calmer voice, "Slip down, honey. This old pony, he's a mite winded."

The pony was worse than winded. He'd been run clear off his feet. He stood now with his head down and his forefeet spraddled. He sucked for air in great gasps. His flanks quivered. Sweat ran in little rivers down the insides of his hind legs, wetting the red sand.

"Who saw them?" Papa asked.

Lisbeth slid from the horse's rump to the ground. She straightened and smoothed down the skirt of her dress. She was maybe thirteen, with long blond hair and big solemn brown eyes that looked at you in a way that always made you feel bashful and awkward.

She looked at me now. I squirmed and looked away toward Mama. I took notice of how white-faced and anxious Mama looked, how she kept wiping her hands on her cooking apron, when they weren't even wet.

"Why, nobody, I reckon," Searcy answered. He pressed forked fingers against his lips and spat tobacco juice into the sand. "Best I could learn, the horses turned up missing at daylight this morning. Fourteen head, belonging to a feller named Buschwaldt." He heaved himself down out of the saddle.

Papa said, "Missing horses don't have to mean Indians. Horses can stray."

"Not them horses," Searcy said. "Buschwaldt said Injuns

got 'em. Told Tom McDougal they did. Tom, he said it sounded like Injuns to him. And you know Tom ain't a man to lie—lessen maybe they's a little money involved."

He turned and handed his bridle reins to Lisbeth.

"Here, honey," he said. "Better go water this old pony. Might shuck him out a few ears of corn, too, while you're at it. Build back his strength to pack us home."

Lisbeth turned to lead the horse off to water. I felt a great relief. Searcy's Indian story didn't sound like much to me. I figured I knew now what he was up to. Searcy made a practice of riding around, peddling tall-tale news. And the price you paid for hearing it was generally a big hearty meal for him and a feed for his horse.

I guess Papa was thinking the same thing, for he looked relieved, too. But Mama didn't.

"Where's Little Arliss?" she said in a tight voice.

"Off in the hills somewhere," I told her. "Him and Sam. Heard Sam on the trail of a varmint not thirty minutes ago."

"Go get him," she said sharply.

I looked into her anxious eyes, then toward Papa. Papa seemed dubious, but nodded his head. "Might be better you did, son," he said. "Till we can get the straight of this."

I turned and headed for the corral to saddle a horse. I was too worn out from brush grubbing to trample all over the hills in the hot sun, hunting Arliss afoot. Behind me, I heard the hurt and anger in Searcy's voice as he flared up at Papa.

"Git the straight of it!" he said hotly. "Well, I'll just tell you a thing, Jim Coates. If you've got a defenseless youngun foot-loose in the hills, the chances are them murdering hostiles has done ketched and sculped him!"

I wished he'd shut up. That sort of scare talk was sure to upset Mama; and I was willing to bet there wasn't a lick of truth in it. But hushing up Bud Searcy was like trying to stop dry leaves from rattling in a high wind. The way he kept his tongue wagging, you'd think it was hinged in the middle and loose at both ends. What talking time he'd lose from now till Mama called us to dinner would be just enough to spit tobacco juice all over the white creek sand we kept spread in the dog run between

5

the two rooms of our cabin. And once at the table, he'd eat and talk till the last scrap of food was gone. After that, he'd go back to talking and spitting more tobacco juice till along in the cool of the evening, when maybe he'd finally saddle up and ride off home, acting like he'd done a big favor by paying us a visit.

My roan horse, Blue, nickered a welcome as I pushed open the corral gate. Our plow mule, Jumper, though, he wheeled and raced to the far side of the corral. There he stood, snorting and stomping the ground with his forefeet, eying me like I was a colt-eating Mexican lion. Jumper was seventeen or eighteen years old, but he did his best to act like he was still the wildest bronc mule that ever jumped from under a set of harness.

In some ways, Jumper had a lot in common with old man Searcy.

I caught Blue and pitched a saddle on him. I was just cinching up the girth when Lisbeth led her grandpa's sweat-lathered pony into the corral.

"Could I go with you, Travis?" she asked.

"Not on that run-down pony," I said. "He's still shaking with the weak trembles."

"I know," Lisbeth said. "But—"

She broke off there without finishing. She stood waiting while I jerked loose the cinch and dragged the saddle from the back of her grandpa's pony. I stripped the bridle over his ears and the bits out of his mouth. Then I turned to the log crib to shuck out some corn for him.

"And that blue roan of mine," I added over my shoulder. "I'm not right sure he's safe to ride double."

Actually, Blue would pack double without turning a hair. But I didn't mind having Lisbeth think the horse I rode was about half dangerous.

She didn't say anything. I looked up from my corn-shucking, and the disappointment in her eyes was plain.

I recollected how I'd hurt Lisbeth's feelings the time she'd brought the six-weeks-old Sam to me as a present. That was when me and Old Yeller had got cut up so bad by a bunch of range hogs. And what with still having a grown dog at the time, I'd told Lisbeth I was too sick to be pestered with a pup right then. So she'd given Sam

6

to Little Arliss and gone off and had herself a good cry about it.

Mama, she learned what I'd done and hopped all over me, fussy as a wet hen, telling me I ought to be ashamed, telling me what a nice, sweet-natured little girl Lisbeth was and how she just worshiped the very ground I walked on. And while I wasn't interested in having anybody worship the ground I walked on, I did, after thinking on it a spell, come to see that Mama was right. When you got down to scratch, you had to admit that—for a girl—Lisbeth was just as fine a person as you could expect to come across in a week's ride.

Now, looking at her, all of a sudden I wanted to take her along.

"Look," I said. "Old Jumper, he won't let your pony eat without trying to rob him. Why don't I just saddle him for you to ride?"

Her eyes lit up. "That'll be fine," she said. "Only, don't bother with a saddle. I'm used to riding bareback."

So I went and tied a catch rope around Jumper's neck. I held down a hand for Lisbeth to step into and boosted her up astride Jumper. I looped a noose of the rope around Jumper's nose, handed the slack end up to her for a guide rein, and she was all fixed. I fed Searcy's pony in a hollow log Papa had split open and made into a feed trough. Then I mounted Blue and we rode out into the hills to search for Little Arliss.

Our part of Texas was a rough country of brushy hogback ridges and rock-bench slopes, with wide mesquite flats and deep-cut canyons and tight little valleys studded with great gnarled live oaks. Willows, pecans, elms, and cottonwoods lined the watercourses.

It was also a country where the weather was generally too hot or too cold, too wet or too dry. But this year had been one of the rare good ones, when the summer rains came heavy and regular, so that now the bluestem grass covered the ground like the shaggy pelt of some huge animal. It stood tall and green as a wheat field, clear to the tops of the highest ridges. The hot sunlight put a glimmer and sheen on the blades as they bowed before the running wind waves.

Ripe prickly-pear apples shone red through the tossing grass. Cenizo bloomed lavendar. And snow-white against the green of the grass drooped long, top-heavy sprays of flowering bee myrtle, filling the air with their sharp, clean fragrance.

Wild bees hummed about the flowers, and I was just recollecting the last bee tree me and Papa had cut when Lisbeth goosed Jumper up beside me.

"Travis," she asked, "you think Grandpa is right? About the Indians, I mean?"

Knowing what a windbag her grandpa was, it would have crowded me to believe there was an Indian in the country if I'd caught one chasing him. Still, I couldn't hardly say that to Lisbeth. So I said, "I don't much think so. Been a long time since Indians raided in these parts. Eight or nine years, best I remember."

Her eyes widened. "You can remember?" she asked.

I could remember, all right. It stuck in my mind like a bad dream you sometimes get after eating a bait of fried hog liver for supper.

. . . Me, lying belly-flat on the puncheon floor under the bed where Papa had shoved me . . . Listening to the thundering reports of the rifles inside and outside the cabin . . . to the hysterical baying of our watchdogs . . . to the scared bawling of the milk cows and their calves . . . to the snorting and whistling of the horses in the corral . . . to the unearthly screeches of the attacking Comanches . . . to the splintering crash of wood, as arrows and rifle balls slammed into the thick logs of our cabin walls . . . to that terrible, lonesome cry of spent bullets wailing off into the brush . . . to the quick footsteps of Papa and old man Mercer and his harelipped boy Dude as they hurried from the porthole windows to hand Mama their empty guns and grab up the ones she'd just reloaded.

Me, lying there, hearing it all and seeing nothing . . . Till, finally, the harelipped boy staggered backward, circled, stumbled against the bed, and went down . . . where I watched his heels drum against the floor boards as he died.

It was no trouble to remember. None at all. But the tell-

8

ing wasn't so easy; and I don't guess I made much of a job of it, because when I got through, all Lisbeth could think of to say was, "Wasn't you scared?"

I told her that I guessed I was—some—but I was quick to point out that I was about the size of Little Arliss at the time, and added that I didn't reckon I'd be so scared now.

"Well, I'd a-been scared," Lisbeth said. "Just pure-dee scared to death!"

Lisbeth's grandpa held the reputation of being the biggest liar in the country. On the other hand, Lisbeth was so open and honest about everything that sometimes she put you to shame.

We rode quiet up a long slant, topped out a high rise, and Lisbeth pulled Jumper to a stop.

"Listen!" she said. "I believe I hear Sam."

I stopped and listened. Sure enough, from across the next rise, I caught the ringing trail cry of Savage Sam. From the sound of it, Sam was driving hard, telling the whole wide world that he had some varmint on the run and was taking it yonder.

This was the main difference between Sam and his papa. Old Yeller had been the worst thief, the biggest glutton, the fiercest fighter, and the greatest old fraud you ever saw. To some extent, Sam had inherited all these traits; but from his mama, he had come up with one thing extra. From his eyes on out to the tip end of his muzzle, Sam was every inch a trail hound. He had a nose on him that wouldn't quit. At the age of seven months, he was done treeing squirrels for Little Arliss, who had to knock them out with rocks because Papa wouldn't let him pack a gun.

By the time Sam was a year old, he'd pick up the trail of a fox or coon and hang it for a two- and three-hour stretch. And always behind him chased Little Arliss, yelling encouragement, just as eager as Sam to bring the varmint to bay, where he'd join in the rowdy battle that was sure to follow.

"Just listen to him," Lisbeth said. "Hasn't he got the prettiest sounding voice? Prettier even than his mama."

Sam had that, all right. Let him open on a trail, and you couldn't keep from listening. High-pitched and far-reaching, his voice held some special quality that left the bell

9

pure notes ringing strong in your ears long after you knew Sam had to be clear out of hearing distance.

Time and again, I'd caught myself stopping whatever work I was doing, just to stand and listen to the sweet wild call of that old pup's trail cry. If Papa happened to be working with me, I noticed that he always stopped to listen, too. Then, pretty soon, he'd grin and shake his head and say, "Savage Sam and Little Arliss! Now, ain't that a pair for you? Wilder than a couple of thicket-raised shoats!"

Then we'd go back to work, maybe hoeing careless weeds out of the young corn. And the hot sun would burn down on my back and the sweat would drip from under my hatbrim, stinging my eyes with salt, and I'd get tired and feel the hoe handle raising a blister inside my hand and get to wishing that Sam would lose his trail and shut up, so I wouldn't have to listen to him and be reminded of how much fun him and Little Arliss were having while I was stuck there in the field, practically working myself to death.

And never once did it enter my head that a time would come when I'd be listening for that wild trail cry of Sam's, clinging to it like it was the last shred of hope left in a world of complete despair.

*Travis*

# Two

WE rode toward Sam's voice. We crossed a wide draw where the grass grew so tall I could touch it with my hand from where I sat in the saddle.

We jumped a little bunch of deer and watched them go racing through the grass with their white tails flared. One was a buck with a spread of antlers the size of a rocking chair—and I hadn't thought to pack along a gun.

We reached the top of the next rise overlooking a deep-cut canyon and pulled up to listen. For a second, we thought we heard Sam's voice. We hunted a break in the wall till we found where a cow trail twisted down through the brush. We followed the trail. It got steeper and rougher the further we went. The brush dragged and rattled against our legs. And what with Blue and Jumper slipping and having to rump-slide down the steepest places, kicking up loose rocks that came clattering down the trail after us, we stirred up a considerable racket and some dust.

Down at the bottom, we stopped to let Blue and Jumper sip seep water out of a pothole in the rocks. For a minute, everything was quiet, and that's when we heard Arliss and Sam again.

The best I could tell, they were no longer trailing a varmint. Sounded more like they had it treed. Only, the sounds were muffled, as if coming up out of a deep well. I wasn't even certain what direction they came from.

Then Blue lifted his head, to chomp his bridle bits and spatter water down on the flat rocks. And when he'd finished, he caught the sound, too, and bent his ears up the canyon. So we rode off in that direction; and sure enough, when we rounded a shoulder of broken rocks, we located Sam and Arliss.

That is, we located the hole they were in.

The mouth of the hole opened under a ledge at the base of a high cliff. The hole was about the size of a barrel, and ran far back into the rocks. Out of the hole came Sam's steady barking and Arliss's excited voice.

"Git him, Sam!" Arliss was urging. "Grab him, boy! Chew him up!"

I stepped down out of my saddle. Behind me, I heard the gravel crunch as Lisbeth's feet hit the ground. I went and stuck my head into the hole and caught the smell of stale dust and the rank scent of some wild animal. It was too dark in there to see anything.

I hollered into the hole. I said, "Arliss! What have y'all got back in there?"

"A bobcat!" Arliss said, all excited.

"A bobcat?" I said. I didn't much believe him.

"You bet!" Arliss said. "A big old tom. I'm poking him with a stick."

He must have poked him again, for I heard the angry snarling of a cat.

"Arliss!" I hollered. "You come back out of that hole!"

"Not till we git this old bobcat," Arliss said.

"You let that bobcat alone!" I said. "You hear me? You get him riled, he's liable to come out of there and eat you alive!"

"He can't come out," Arliss said. "Me 'n' old Sam, we're in here so tight, we got his hole stoppered up!"

That pesky Arliss. Trying to reason with him was like butting your head against a stooping post oak.

"Looks like I'll have to go in there after him," I told Lisbeth, and went crawling back into the hole.

I could hear Arliss and Sam and the bobcat scratching and scrambling around. I could hear them hollering and barking and growling. They were stirring up enough dust to choke a gray mule and making such a racket you couldn't hear yourself think.

The further in I crawled, the smaller the hole got. Finally, I was lying flat on my belly, squeezed in so tight that I shut out all the light. I couldn't go any further; all I could do was feel around in the dark till I located one of Arliss's rusty bare feet. I took a good tight grip on his ankle and went to backing out.

Arliss threw a conniption fit. "You turn me a-loose, Travis Coates!" he railed at me. "You don't turn me a-loose, I'll bust you with a rock!"

He'd have done it, too, if there'd been room enough. Any time Arliss threatened you with a rock, you'd better duck. Like it was, though, the best he could do was kick me in the mouth a couple of times with his free foot before he set it against the wall of the cave, bracing himself against my pull. Then I couldn't budge him.

Well, I'd pulled enough armadillos out of holes to beat him at that game.

You take an armadillo. You ever let him get set in a hole with all four feet braced against the sides, it'd take a yoke of oxen to yank him out. On the other hand, you can set back on his horny tail with a steady pull—not straining, but just keeping a steady pressure on him—and after a while, you'll feel his legs give a little. Then you know you've got him.

That's how I got Arliss. I just let him scream and threaten me with murder while I kept a steady pull on his one leg. When finally I felt the other leg start quivering, I gave a hard yank and slid him back out of that hole like he'd been greased with tallow.

He came out fighting, and the first glimpse I got of his dirty, tear-streaked face made me wish I'd dragged out the bobcat instead. I barely ducked in time to keep him from busting my head open with a fist-sized rock.

I grabbed and held Arliss's rock hand and yelled at him to behave himself, while he screamed at me to turn him loose. And we were still down on our hands and knees, scrambling around, when Sam and the big bobcat came waltzing out into the open, all wrapped up in each other's arms.

They landed right on top of me and Little Arliss, roaring and snarling, clawing and biting. I flung myself one way and Arliss went the other. But as fast and furious as Sam and that bobcat fought, they were all over both of us two or three times while we were still trying to get from under.

Once, they caught me flat on my back with my mouth

open, and Sam shoved a hind foot down my throat clear up to the hock, it seemed like, before he jerked it back out.

I was yelling and Arliss was yelling and Lisbeth was screaming and Blue and Jumper were shying around, whistling and snorting and popping the rocks with their ironshod hoofs, so that altogether it was a right noisy and exciting fight.

When finally I got to my feet, I saw right off what Sam was learning gradually: he had overmatched himself. That big bobcat was ripping him to pieces.

Well, Sam was nobody's fool. He'd been in enough scraps to know when he was licked. The first chance he got to cut loose from the cat, he took it. He tucked his tail and came running toward me and Arliss, bawling for help.

That should have ended the fight. But by now, this old bobcat was so fuzzed-up mad, he wasn't satisfied to call it quits. He charged after Sam with his teeth bared, his yellow eyes glaring, and his ears flattened to his head. He was still out for blood, and it didn't seem to matter whose blood it was. The instant Sam swept around to get behind me, I was the next handiest thing in reach; so the cat sprang at me.

All I had time to do was give him a good hard kick. This shook him, but not enough. He caught my leg and clung to it and began clawing and biting as fiercely as he'd worked on Sam.

I went stumbling backward and sat down with a jolt that rattled my teeth. I went to yelling again and kicking at the bobcat with my other foot. I wasn't doing much good, though, and I guess the bobcat would have soon had me chewed up worse than Sam if it hadn't been for Arliss moving in, swinging the big rock he'd meant to bust me with.

Arliss was little for his age; but put a throwing rock in his hand, and he got bigger in a hurry. Now, he cut down on this bobcat with all he had. He laid that rock up against the rascal's head so hard that it addled him. You never saw such wallowing and pitching and squawling and leaping as that bobcat did. It was worse than the fits a game rooster will pull off after you've wrung his neck.

I came to my feet. Blue snorted loud. Sam came charging

past me with his hackles raised, barking furiously. I looked around and felt my heart stop cold.

*Indians!*

They were all around us.

Some were mounted. Others were leaping from their horses and racing toward us, brandishing rifles and long lances.

All this I saw in one quick flash, just as a loop of hair rope came swishing through the air and dropped down around me.

The loop was jerked shut with a force that pinned my arms to my sides and yanked me off my feet. I hit the ground hard. I heard Lisbeth scream, then Little Arliss. A second later, I screamed, too, as I felt myself being dragged across the canyon bed at a speed that had me bouncing over the rocks.

The rocks cut and banged me and scraped the hide off in chunks. Then my head slammed against one and everything went black except for a great shower of pin-wheeling stars.

When I came to, I was nearly as addled as the bobcat had been. The ground rocked and heaved. The high canyon wall leaned out over me, then swayed back in the other direction. But gradually my head cleared and I was able to take note of what was going on.

I found myself astride a big rawboned bay horse. My shirt and hat were gone. My hands were tied behind me. A big tall Indian with long ropes of hair down his back was lashing my feet against the bay's ribs with a strip of rawhide pulled up tight under the horse's belly. The bay was snorting and lunging sideways, but couldn't do much, on account of a squat Indian swinging to his head. This Indian had a leg and one arm hooked over the bay's neck. He held a tight-handed grip on the bay's underjaw, and had his teeth clamped shut over one ear. Most of his weight swung from that ear.

I tried to kick free, but the tall Indian's grip on my foot was too tight. A second later, he had my feet bound. He grunted to the squat Indian, who released his grip on the horse and dropped free. The bay snorted, ran backward a few steps, then bogged his head and went to bawling and pitching.

Well, I'd tried my hand a few times at riding pitching horses. But I'd never done it scared to death, like now, with my hands tied behind me and my feet pulled so tight against a horse's ribs that there was no give anywhere. The first jump whipped my head back, and the jolt I got when he hit the ground shot a stab of pain up my spine. I couldn't seem to stiffen my neck, and after that, just had to ride limp, with my head snapping back and forth like the popper on a bullwhip.

If the bay had kept pitching, he would have broken my neck. But he was more scared than mean. He didn't make more than a half a dozen jumps before he went piling into a band of some fifty other horses held against a crook in the canyon wall by a couple of mounted Indians. There, he threw up his head and quit pitching. He shied around till he stood with the others, all stomping their feet and whistling wild.

For the first time, then, I got to see what was happening to Lisbeth and Little Arliss.

Both had been caught. Lisbeth was already mounted in front of an Indian with a broken nose. He held her tight against him with a hand clamped over her mouth. All I could see of her face was her big scared eyes.

With Arliss, though, things were different. A short-coupled Indian had hold of him. He'd caught up a fistful of Arliss's shaggy hair and had the strength to swing Arliss's heels clear of the ground. But he still lacked some having Arliss captured.

This was because every time he yanked the screaming Arliss up close enough, Arliss either kicked him or hammered him with a big rock he'd somehow got his hands on.

Also, there was Sam.

I'd never seen Sam so savage before. I'd never seen him attack with such deadly fury. It was plain that he didn't look on this fight as a big romp, like he and Arliss had just pulled off with the bobcat. This wasn't the sort of scrap that Sam would turn tail to any time the going got too rough.

Sam saw this for what it was: a kill-or-be-killed proposition. And no naked wild man was going to sling Sam's running partner around by the hair of the head so long as Sam could do anything about it. Sam tore into the Indian with his eyes glazed and his hackles standing in a ragged ridge along his backbone. His fangs cut bloody grooves in the Indian's neck and shoulders.

So with Sam and Arliss teaming up on him like that, the squat Indian was kept right busy—and with nobody to help him out.

Because not one of the others offered to take a hand in the fight. Instead, they stood off and watched and yelped with laughter. From the tone of their voices, they made hoorawing remarks and waited to see how it would all come out. Like the whole thing was a great big joke.

There for a little bit, it looked like Sam and Arliss might win. For Sam made another leap, sank his teeth into the Indian's neck, and took him to the ground. But the fall broke Sam's grip. The Indian rolled instantly to his feet. Pitching Arliss aside, he snatched a tomahawk from his belt. Sam wheeled and charged again—and the Indian chopped him down.

The stone blade caught Sam in the back. It sent him screeching, leaving a trail of blood as he wallowed down a rocky slant in a frenzy of pain. He disappeared behind some great shards of rock. And before he was out of sight, the Indian had whirled and caught Arliss again. He bent and grabbed him by a leg this time. Holding him upside down and out away from him, he strode quickly toward his horse.

All the other Indians now turned toward their mounts. Some of the horses they mounted wore bridles and forked-stick saddles covered over with buffalo hides. Others were barebacked and had only single strips of rawhide half-hitched around their underjaws to serve as guide reins.

As scared and stunned as I was, I couldn't help taking notice of how easily those naked savages mounted up. No matter how a boogered horse might lunge or shy around, the Indian that meant to ride him would just make a quick running jump and land astride before the horse could get from under.

The only one to miss was the big tall Indian who had captured me. He'd just made a leap at his horse when I heard him grunt. I saw him whirl in mid-air and tumble to

17

the ground as if slapped down by a heavy blow. Then I heard the crashing report of a rifle coming from far back up on the ridge.

Instantly, the tall Indian bounded to his feet, clutching at a blood-spurting hole inside his right leg. All the others took wild looks around, then went to whooping and screeching, lashing their mounts, circling to get behind the whistling band of loose horses and scare them into a run.

The rifle spoke again. The bullet glanced off a rock and went screaming away. I twisted around, trying to see who was doing the shooting, and nearly got my head snapped off again as the big bay made a sudden leap and went tearing off down the canyon bed, running wild with the rest of the loose horses.

I never did hear the third shot. There was too much whooping and yelling, too much hoof-popping clatter, too many echoes slamming back and forth between the canyon walls. All I saw was a running horse stumble and go down. His rider leaped from his back and ran beside him as the fallen horse slid forward with his outstretched nose rooting a furrow in a sand bed. Then a loose horse came by and the Indian leaped astride and went to drumming his heels against this horse's ribs, urging him to greater speed.

We rode at a stampede run down the rocky bed of the twisting canyon. I looked around for Lisbeth and Arliss. I didn't see Lisbeth, but the glimpse I caught of Arliss made me sick.

To the left and a little behind me rode the squat Indian. He still held Arliss by one heel. Every stitch of clothes had been torn from Arliss's body. He swung, head down, beside the running horse, with the thorny brush raking his naked hide.

I thought to myself: *His head ever strikes a tree or a boulder, it'll kill him.*

We went crashing through a grove of Spanish oak. An outspread branch slapped the side of my head. I bent forward and laid my cheek against the bay's neck so I could shed the brush better. But I couldn't see any more of what was happening to Little Arliss or Lisbeth.

*Apache*

# Three

WE RACED north, following the crooks and turns of the canyon. We traveled at a dead run; and in some places, the bed of the watercourse, was so rough and jumbled with boulders, I didn't see how the horses kept on their feet.

Finally, the canyon walls began to fan out, spreading wider and wider, till at last there were only sweeping slopes slanting away from the creek. Here, the Indians swung the racing herd up the slope to the west, still driving at the same killing pace.

There were no trees on this slope, except for a few gnarled mesquite and now and then a round-topped live oak. The rest was just brush—catclaw, chapote, bluethorn, tasajillo cactus, prickly pear, and bee myrtle. None of it was more than horse high. It tore at my legs, but there was no danger of its knocking me from my horse. I raised my head and took another look around.

Off to one side, I saw Little Arliss again, still held by one foot, but now lying head down across the lap of the Indian who had caught him. He lay limp and jostling, like he was dead. But I guessed he must still be alive. Why else would the Apache keep packing him?

Lisbeth was still being held upright in her captor's saddle. He wasn't holding his hand over her mouth anymore, but her face was dead white, and the terrible fear I saw in her eyes kindled in me a fire of hate that flared hotter and fiercer with every mile of ground we covered. She looked toward me once, and I saw her mouth move, but I couldn't hear her voice.

I was helpless now. They had me bound hand and foot.

If they were smart, that's the way they'd keep me, too. Because, if I ever got loose and got my hands on the red devils who held Lisbeth and Arliss, I'd claw their eyes out. I'd choke them to death. I'd hammer their heads in with a rock or rip their bellies open with my pocketknife. And if one of them finally chopped me down, like that one had done Savage Sam, that would be all right, too—just so I got some of them first!

We went tearing on through the brush, but the slant was long and tiring to the running horses. Some began to lag. I saw Jumper running at the outside of the herd. He still wore the frazzled leavings of his rope, but he'd trampled most of it to pieces under his feet. I could see him edging further and further off. I knew in a minute what he was up to, and I hoped he got away.

But one of the Indians saw him, too, and went charging past and stabbed him in the rump with a lance. This put more life into Jumper than I'd seen him show for a long time. He spurted forward, wringing his tail and braying, slinging his high-held head from side to side, traveling at a pace that soon had him leading the bunch.

He put on such a silly show that he set all the Indians to pointing and laughing as they dashed back and forth through the brush, prodding the stragglers into a faster run.

Out of the tail of my eye, I caught a glimpse of the big tall Indian who'd been shot. He rode my horse, Blue. He stood off in the left stirrup, trying to favor the bullet wound inside his right leg. He held a hand clamped over the wound to keep it from rubbing against the saddle. Blood seeped from between his fingers, staining his buckskin leggings and spreading down over the saddle skirts. From the way he rode, he must have been suffering a lot from that wound.

I thought to myself: *Maybe he'll bleed to death.* That would cheer me some.

He looked up and caught my eye on him. I don't guess he could read what I was thinking, but something about my look seemed to give him an idea.

He spanked Blue across the rump with his lance, crowding him up beside me. He looped the bridle reins around the saddle horn so they couldn't drop to the ground and maybe trip and throw Blue. Then he leaped from the sad-

20

dle, grabbed me by the foot, and went running beside me.

We had topped out the rise by this time. Now, headed downhill, the horses—even the stragglers—picked up speed, so that again we went charging along at a pace that made a blur of the brush and the ground beneath me.

How that tall Indian could hold to my foot and keep pace with the rawboned bay I rode, I'll never know. But he did it, crashing through or ducking under the taller brush, leaping lightly over the clumps of prickly pear and tasajillo, never once faltering, never once dragging at my foot, never once really breaking his stride, which was as long-reaching and smooth-flowing as that of a running cat.

I could ride there beside him and hate him. I could tell myself that I hoped he bled to death before sundown. But watching him run like he did, I couldn't help marveling. He might be a cruel, merciless savage, but he was all man.

Watching him, I took note of the fact that he was different from the others. As I've said, he was taller and better built than his heavyset companions. On top of that, where all the others wore streaks of white paint from ear to ear across the bridges of their noses, this one had his whole face covered with slanted stripes of black and red. Where they were naked from breechclouts down to peak-toed moccasins except for wrap-around leggings reaching nearly to their knees, this one wore fringed buckskin breeches that covered him from feet to waist, except for holes in the seat that left bare the rounded cheek muscles of his rump. Also, he wore fringed and beaded moccasins of tanned snakeskin—rattlesnake, from the brown diamond pattern marks —with the tails of ground squirrels attached to the heels.

The main difference, however, was the way he wore his hair. The others had their hair parted in the middle and chopped off to shoulder length. Some wore colored headbands of twisted cloth to hold their hair in place, and some wore their hair braided into tight little pigtails that flipped around behind their ears.

My big Indian, though, had two parts in his hair, with a streak of yellow marking each part. The parts ran from each side of his forehead back to the crown, leaving a V-shaped forelock into which he'd stuck a long yellow feather. From there on, his hair hung in two long cowtail twists,

21

wrapped at intervals with yellow string, till finally they were left to flare in six-inch tassels that all but brushed the ground. As he ran, these cowtails flopped and whipped about like scared snakes in tall grass.

Something about those ropes of hair fascinated me. I kept watching them. I kept telling myself that no man, even a wild Indian, could grow hair that long. And finally, I saw that I was right. Only about a foot and a half of it was his. The rest was horsetail hair that he'd braided into his own to make the tails longer.

From what I'd heard Papa and others tell of Plains Indians, I judged this big one to be Comanche. He was tall for a Comanche, but he wore Comanche garb. The peak-toed moccasins marked the others as Apache. How come a lone Comanche was raiding with a bunch of Apaches, I didn't know; but it wasn't a question to bother with now. My worry was how to get me and Lisbeth and Little Arliss away from the painted-faced devils.

That job would fall to me, and I knew it. Arliss—if he was still alive—was too little; and Lisbeth—well, she was just a girl.

But how to go about it? That's what had me plagued. How could a sixteen-year-old boy whip or outsmart fifteen wild Indians? And him tied hand and foot?

Then I thought about the man who'd shot from the top of the ridge. Whoever he was, he'd get the word out. He'd hurry to Salt Licks and round up Papa and some of the settlers, and they'd be on our trail in no time.

That lifted my hopes. There were some crack rifle shots and experienced Indian hunters at Salt Licks.

One of them went by the name of Burn Sanderson. Sanderson was a good friend of ours. He'd been the one to let us have Old Yeller when Papa was gone and we'd been in such desperate need of a watchdog. Old Yeller had been Sanderson's best cow dog, yet he'd swapped him off to Little Arliss for a horned toad and a good home-cooked meal that Mama fixed up for him.

Sanderson had ridden for the Texas Rangers and was a real Indian tracker. Papa claimed Sanderson could track wild bees in a blizzard, that he would hang an Indian trail like a bloodhound.

22

Thinking of Papa and Sanderson taking our trail sent a warm feeling through me, yet I wondered if even Sanderson could work out our trail fast enough to overhaul us.

We raced on through the hills. The wild things scattered and fled before us. Cottontails streaked for the nearest brush cover. So did the deer. Jack rabbits took to the open places, depending on speed for safety. Once, the running horses shied at a big covey of bob-white quail that exploded under their noses. Another time, the band split and streamed past on both sides of a black she-bear, who rose to stand on her hinds legs. She roared a warning at them to keep away from the pair of whimpering cubs at her heels. We jumped a couple of long-bearded wild gobblers. They saddle-trotted ahead of us for a little way, then took to the air with heavy wing beats.

Where the ground was bare and rocky, the thudding hoofbeats of the horses were like thunder in my ears. When we struck a wide mesquite flat, the sound of our passing faded, the hoofbeats muffled by the thick, matted turf of the tall-waving grass. But no matter what sort of country we crossed, we kept traveling at the same horse-killing pace.

The horse I rode became lathered with sweat. The sweat soaked through my pants, stinging and galling the flesh of my legs, which were already rubbed raw from being bound so tight to the bay's back. My head throbbed from the blows it had taken among the rocks. The hot sun burned down on my naked shoulders till I knew I'd be on fire with sunburn before night.

I thought of Little Arliss, stripped naked. I wondered if he'd sunburn, too, but guessed he wouldn't. His skin was tougher. He was used to running around naked in hot weather and having Mama fuss at him for not being decent.

I guessed Mama wouldn't fuss at him now. I guessed that by now, she was clear out of her mind with worry for us all, praying to get us back, even if she knew Arliss would run naked as a summer-hatched chicken for the rest of his life.

I looked toward Arliss. He still lay limp across the saddle. But now he was watching his captor out of the corners of his eyes.

23

I'd seen that look before. Arliss was studying up some sort of devilment.

It was good to know he was that much alive. But it scared me, too. I hoped he'd hold off starting a ruckus till I could get free to help him out.

We rode till the sun sank behind the ridges, its last rays setting fire to the underbelly of a thunderhead that threatened rain. We topped out a high, rocky, cedar-covered ridge and went plunging down a long slant toward the Llano River. In the fading light the water looked like gold running between red rock banks. When we got closer, the gold grayed to silver.

We hit the river where the banks were high and the water looked deep. Downstream, I could see the ripple of shoal water flowing over a shallow bottom where the crossing would have been easy; but if the Indians saw the shallow water, they paid it no mind. They kept driving straight ahead.

At the bank, some of the horses tried to shy away from a ten-foot jump-off. But the Indians came racing up on either side. With whoops and lashes, they sent the horses plunging over the bank into water so deep that the bay I rode sank clear under.

I thought I was a goner, for sure, when the water closed over my head. But in a little bit, the bay rose to the surface and struck out for the far bank, swimming like he was used to it.

I missed the grip of the big Indian's hand on my foot. I looked around, half blinded by the water streaming down out of my hair. I hoped the big devil had got knocked down by a scared horse and trampled to death.

But luck was against me. There he was, alive as ever, hanging to the tail of the swimming bay with one hand, holding onto his lance with the other.

I noticed him looking downriver and grinning. It came to me then that all the other Indians were hollering and laughing. I looked across the backs of a lot of swimming horses and saw a sight that set my heart to flopping around like a catfish in a wet sack.

It was Arliss. On the fight again!

24

Like I'd suspected a good ways back, he'd been playing possum, waiting to get a break. Now, something must have happened to give him that break. For there he was, all balled up on that Indian's head like a boar coon fighting a trail hound.

He had a bare foot planted firm on each of the Indian's shoulders. He had a tight grip with both hands on the Indian's hair. But what counted most was the fact that he had a mouthful of the rascal's left ear between his teeth and was setting back on it, shaking and tugging for all he was worth, doing his dead-level best to tear that ear out by the roots.

The howling Apache fought back. He hammered the side of Arliss's head with his fist. He slapped his face. He pulled his hair. He grabbed him by one foot and tried to yank him loose. But nothing did any good. The way Arliss kept his teeth set in that ear put me in mind of what I'd always heard tell about a snapper turtle—that once he shuts his jaws down on your finger, he won't turn loose till it thunders. Anyhow, all the yanking and tugging the Apache did only helped Arliss to pull that much harder on his ear.

With all this, the Apache was having trouble with his horse. The horse was scared. The way he kept lunging up to paw at the surface with his forefeet, it was plain that he'd never been in swimming water. Then there was all this racket and commotion on his back. And worst of all, with Arliss riding clear up on the Apache's head, the load was topheavy and kept pulling the horse off balance.

So, while the Apache fought Arliss on top of his head, he was kept just as busy shifting his weight, trying to keep his horse right side up in the water.

Altogether, it was too much for the horse. I saw that he was never going to make it.

"Turn him loose, Arliss!" I yelled.

If Arliss heard, he paid me no more mind than he generally did. The horse rolled over and went under. Arliss and the Apache sank with him, with the Apache still fighting at Arliss and Arliss still clinging grimly to his ear hold.

Relieved of his load, the horse rose to the surface almost at once. He got footing where the water shallowed, and went lunging and scrambling over the rock bottom toward the bank.

Arliss and the Apache stayed under longer, so long that it scared me. Then the Apache came up without Arliss. Also without his ear. All he had left of that ear was a ragged stump that spewed blood down the side of his neck and reddened the water about his shoulders.

He held there where he came up, treading water and looking around in fury, searching for Arliss.

The other Indians hooted at him. They pulled at their ears to show that they still had theirs and kept pointing to the Apache's bloody stump.

It was plain that none of this pleased the wounded Apache, and I sure hoped that when Arliss came to the top —if he ever did—he'd be out of reach of that Indian.

And he was. I'd heard Papa declare that when it came to swimming, all Arliss lacked being a fish was a couple of gill slits and a forked tail. When his head finally popped out of the water, he was close to the far bank, swimming among the lead horses.

The Apache saw him at once and struck out after him, swimming fast. But Arliss beat him to the bank and went out into the flat-rock ledge among the slipping, scrambling horses.

Then my bay struck bottom and went buck-jumping up a slick rock slant toward dry ground, and for a second there, I lost sight of Arliss. When next I saw him, he was clear of the plunging horses and racing toward me along the rock ledge, yelling at the top of his voice, "Don't let him git me, Travis! Don't let him git me!"

I sure didn't blame him for being scared; for hard after him came the furious Indian. He had his tomahawk raised, and there was a murderous glare in his black eyes.

I was frantic to save Arliss, but couldn't think up any way to do it. All I could do was yell at him, *"Run, Arliss, run!"* Which was silly, because Arliss was running faster than I'd ever seen him run in his life.

But it wasn't fast enough. The Apache was gaining on him with every step he took, and I heard Lisbeth scream.

From behind the bay stepped the tall Comanche. He grabbed Arliss by the hair and slung him up astride the bay horse behind me. He turned, grinning, to poke his lance out toward the charging Apache. The murdering devil all but ran himself through on the point of the lance before he could get stopped.

He backed up with an angry shout. From the way he flung up his tomahawk, I could see he aimed to go to war with the Comanche. But he changed his mind pretty quick when the Comanche moved toward him, drawing back his lance for a throw.

From there on, they aired their lungs with jabber talk that got louder and hotter by the second. The other Indians came to crowd around and take the Comanche's side of the argument. They jeered at the one-eared Apache till finally he wheeled away, his mouth twisted with rage. He stalked off toward his horse and with a running jump landed astride the animal. He lashed him cruelly across the rump and sent him scrambling up the rock-bench slope toward higher ground.

The others then rounded up the scattered horses, and we were on the move again, but no longer at such breakneck speed. We jogged along in the afterglow of the sunset. And, while the Comanche's grip on my foot was as iron tight as ever, it felt good to have Little Arliss behind me with his arms around my waist.

After a while, he said in a worried whisper, "Travis, you reckon I'll be part Injun now?"

"Whatta you mean?" I said.

"That rascal's ear," he said. "I et it."

I started, twisted around to look back at him. "You *what?*"

"Well, I didn't aim to!" he defended. "But I stayed under too long and had to suck for air. And when I did, I got a bellyful of water—and I swallered that ear whole."

It must have been nerves that did it. This sure wasn't any time or place for laughing. But I couldn't help myself. I laughed right out loud and kept on laughing till the tears came and the Indians began moving in close to watch me, curious and puzzled.

If, like Papa was always saying, a big laugh is better for your health than a strong dose of medicine, I was lucky to get in such a good one when I did. As it turned out, I had a long way to go before I was to get another one.

27

*Comanche*

# Four

WE crossed a sharp ridge and clattered down into a tight little valley. More than half the valley was encircled by walls of red sandstone. At one place, huge live oaks and elms grew at the base of the cliff and leaned their branches out over a small pool of water. A bunch of wild longhorn cattle, mostly cows and calves, were gathered at the pool. One or two were still on their feet, drinking; the rest lay on the grassy bank, chewing their cuds, done bedded down for the night.

Our appearance startled the cattle. They scrambled to their feet. The old cows gave loud sniffs, tossed widespread horns, and quit the water hole in a rattle-hocked run. The calves fled after them, holding their tails curled high over their backs.

Instantly, all the Indians except my Comanche and Lisbeth's Apache went chasing after the cattle. They fitted feathered arrows into their bows as they rode.

One chunky mustard-colored calf wasn't as fast as the others. The lead Apache raced up beside it and let fly. His arrow drove clear through the calf's rib cage, the bloody point sticking out three inches on the other side. The calf blatted, and its heels flew high as it tumbled to the ground.

One cow—the calf's mama, I guess—heard the calf and wheeled about. She headed straight for the lead Apache, whose horse hadn't slowed yet. She charged to meet the horse, with her tail crooked and wicked horns lowered. She bawled her wrath.

The Apache was one who rode with a single guide rein. Now, he all but yanked his horse's underjaw out of socket, trying to haul him around. The horse reared, squealing, spun on his hind feet, but lost his balance. Down he came, all in a doubled-up heap.

This would have caught most riders under him, but the Apache was too nimble. He was clear of his fallen horse and running almost before his feet touched the ground. Which was sure lucky for him. Because this old mama cow wasn't bluffing. The horse was up on his forefeet, lifting his rump from the ground, when she hit him. She drove long, sharp horns hard into his shoulders, knocking him back to the ground. The horse screamed and rolled, and the cow hit him again, sinking her horns to the hilt in his soft belly. There she held him, pawing and bawling, trying to drive the horns deeper.

The other Apaches charged up to fill her with arrows and to drive their long lances into her sides and back. But the old cow died slow and hard and not before she'd gored to death the horse she evidently thought was responsible for the death of her calf.

Most of this, me and Arliss watched from the back of the bay horse as he stood in the water hole, drinking in great gulps. Like the others, he'd been kept going at a hard run for most of a long, hot day, with never a chance for a drink, even when we crossed the river. So, when the mounted Apaches pulled off to go shoot the calf, the loose horses had kept going till they reached the water hole. There they had plunged in belly-deep, drinking like they couldn't get enough.

Out on the bank, the Comanche and the Apache who held Lisbeth stood watching the others. Now, one of the Apaches dropped the loop of his rope over the hind leg of the dead calf and came riding toward us, dragging the calf through the tall grass at a fast run. The others followed, leaving the dead cow and the horse where they lay.

At the water's edge, the hunters slid from their horses and came to drink, too.

Well, the water hadn't been much to begin with—just a seep hole, with patches of green scum and slimy frog eggs floating on top and all sorts of tadpoles and bugs and wriggling water worms underneath. And, what with the way the horses had plunged in, trampling around and pawing up the bottom ooze, the water sure didn't look fit to drink.

But none of this bothered the Indians. They tore up fistfuls of grass, wadded it, and laid it on the surface of the water. They lay flat and drank through these grass strainers till they got their fill, then got up and went to butcher the calf.

The way they ripped into that calf's belly with their knives and the parts of it they ate raw was a sight to gag a snake.

Even Arliss, who would generally eat anything he could get his hands on, sneered at them.

"Nasty as buzzards, ain't they?" he said.

The Apache with the broken nose dragged Lisbeth over and tried to make her eat some of the entrails, but she turned sick-white in the face and tried to throw up.

This made the Apache mad. He slapped her flat of her back. He bent and grabbed her by one arm and dragged her over to the water hole. There, he shoved her face under. When she lifted it, strangling and coughing, he shoved it under again.

I thought he was going to drown her. I shouted at him, near to crying with helpless rage.

"You let her alone!"

Little Arliss jumped down off the horse. He ran splashing through the dirty water toward the bank. He grabbed up a rock and drew it back for a throw, threatening the Apache in a shrill voice.

"You quit that!" he demanded. "You don't quit that, I'll bust you with this here rock!"

That stopped the ugly Apache from mistreating Lisbeth.

It wasn't the threat of Little Arliss's rock, of course. In fact, the Apache didn't pay as much attention to that rock as he might ought to have. What stopped him was the sight of Arliss standing there, stark naked, with that big rock in his hand and looking so little and so fierce.

The sight seemed to tickle the Apache. His round face split in a wide grin. He turned Lisbeth loose and started backing off, making such a big show of how scared of Little Arliss he was that he set all the other Indians to laughing.

By now, most of the horses had drunk their fill. They started wading out of the water, headed for graze. The bay I rode started to follow. He was met at the bank by the Comanche, who reached out with a bloody knife and cut the rawhide thong that bound my feet.

I felt the sting of the keen blade as it also sliced on through into my leg. But the cut was shallow, and by now I was hurting in so many places, one little extra pain made no difference.

The Comanche motioned me to dismount, and I lifted a sore leg over the bay's neck and slid down off his shoulder. After so many hours of riding bound, my legs were numb. They buckled under me, and I pitched to the ground.

The Comanche yanked me to my feet. Lisbeth came to hold me steady till the blood got to circulating again. I told her I wanted water. She helped me to get down and stretch out where I could reach it and got a wad of grass for me to drink through.

I'll never forget that drink. Dirty and scummy as the water was, when it hit my parched throat, it seemed like the freshest, sweetest-tasting stuff I'd ever swallowed.

After I'd drunk, Lisbeth and Arliss helped me to my feet. The Comanche had walked off and left us. A few steps away, a big boulder stuck up out of the grass not far from a couple of cottonwood trees. I staggered toward it, dragging the long strip of rawhide still tied to my left foot. I sat down in the shade and leaned against the flat, slanting side of the boulder, making myself as comfortable as I could. Lisbeth and Arliss came to sit, silent and scared, beside me.

It crossed my mind that it was shameful for Little Arliss to go around naked in front of Lisbeth; but I guessed Lisbeth realized that in our fix, clothes didn't amount to a heap.

The Indians paid us no mind. The gloom of the coming

night was fast filling the tiny valley. The savages wound up their first filthy feast, then got busy doing the things that needed to be done before full dark shut in.

A couple started skinning out the calf and chunking up the meat, piling it onto the spread-out hide. Two more went to catch up and hobble the saddled horses. They didn't bother to remove the saddles. One dragged up a long crooked branch of dead mesquite. He broke this into short lengths by beating the pole across a boulder. He gathered up the shattered pieces and carried them to a little sand bed beside the water. There he laid them out fan-shaped, like the spokes of a wagon wheel. Another Indian came and set the flared skirt of a dead bear-grass clump in the center, where the hub of the wheel would have been. In his other hand, he carried a long bear-grass bloom stalk, which was also dead.

While I sat there watching, my mind seemed to split and go off in two directions.

One part was hard at work figuring out a plan of escape. When full dark came, I'd get Lisbeth to untie my hands. We'd watch till the Indians all went to sleep. Then we'd sneak out among the grazing horses. We'd pick the three fastest ones: my horse, Blue; the bay I'd been tied to; and a big rangy glass-eyed paint that one of the Apaches rode. They'd be easy to catch, on account of how tired they had to be. We'd mount up, start yelling to stampede the rest of the horses—and be a long time gone!

The other half of my mind centered on how the savages aimed to get a fire started. Lisbeth's grandpa, who claimed to know all about Indians, along with everything else, had once told me and Arliss how Indians built their fires. He said they half-hitched a tight bowstring around a pointed stick. By moving the bow back and forth, they could twirl the stick so fast that the point of it, pressed down into spunk wood, would set the wood on fire.

Me and Arliss had to try it, but by the time we got our fire-making outfit rigged up, old man Searcy had eaten and gone; so we tried it alone. All we ever raised, though, was a big sweat, some blisters on our hands, and not even one little wisp of smoke.

As it turned out, these Indians didn't bother with a bowstring. Instead, the one with the dead bear-grass stalk took his knife and cut the stalk into a couple of sticks about two feet long. He whittled slanted notches near the ends of each stick, then spilled a fistful of dry sand into the notches. He squatted down on his hunkers and went to rubbing the notched ends together.

He rubbed fast, stopping now and then to spill more sand into the notches. Finally, the ends of the sticks went to smoking, and he shoved them under the bladed skirt of the bear-grass clump. He continued to rub, and smoke curled up faster. The second Apache got down on his hands and knees and blew on the place till it glowed. When he blew again, the glow got brighter, and sparks flew. On the third try, the whole clump burst into flame. The yellow smoke boiled high, and I scented the foul stench that burning bear grass gives off, on account of the oil in the blades.

I watched the Apaches pile small sticks and pieces of shattered bark on the fire to keep it going. I guessed now I could tell old man Searcy a thing or two about Indian fire-making.

Lisbeth whispered, "You want I should untie your hands?"

"Not yet," I said. "Wait till dark."

"I wish we was back to home!" Arliss said.

The whimper and longing in his voice didn't sound like the Arliss who'd fought like a wildcat when captured, who'd eaten one Apache's ear and stood off another with a rock. But I knew how he felt. No matter how wide a boy likes to range in the daytime, when night comes on, he wants to be home, where he can sleep in his own bed and feel safe with his own folks. Especially if he's a little boy. As big as I was, I still had the same feeling a lot of the time. Right now, I had it plenty strong.

"You wait," I told him. "We'll get back home!"

"How?" he wanted to know.

"I got plans," I said.

There wasn't a doubt in my mind but what my plans would work.

The bear-grass clump burned down till its stench was gone. The Apaches brought up their hide-load of meat for cooking. Some of the chunks they laid on flat rocks which they shoved up close to the fire. Most of the meat, however, they just pitched right onto the glowing coals, where it started sizzling and frying.

Watching the fire-making, I'd forgotten the Comanche. Now, I saw him come in out of the gathering darkness. In one hand, he packed a wad of some sort of green weeds. In the other, he carried a small brass pot. He filled the pot with water and set it near the fire. He rolled the weeds between his hands, crushing and bruising them. The weeds filled the air with a rank, sharp scent that reminded me of crushed bull nettles. Then he dropped the weeds into the pot of water.

The Comanche sat down facing the fire and spread his knees wide apart. He bent over to examine the gun-shot wound inside his leg. He slipped his knife from his belt and cut a foot-long slit in his buckskin breeches and spread the slit. In the firelight, I could see the bloody hole in his flesh. A few inches away, a bluish lump stood up under the skin. The Comanche pressed the sides of this lump between thumb and forefinger, making it stand higher, then sliced across the lump. The blood spurted. The Comanche laid aside his knife. He dug a finger into the gaping wound and gouged out the rifle ball lodged there. He wiped it clean on his breeches leg and held it up to examine it by the firelight.

The other Indians crowded around, wanting a look at the ball. The Comanche handed it to one. They all took turns examining it, while the Comanche lifted his weeds out of the brass pot and held them pressed against the wounds in his leg. I guessed they were some sort of medicine weed.

After a while, the Apaches lost interest in the rifle ball. One of them tossed it to the Comanche, who put it away in a little doeskin pouch at his belt.

The Indians lifted the sizzling meat from the fire on the blades of their knives and blew on it to cool it off. When they ate, they didn't cut off slices and put them into their mouths. Instead, they bit into the whole chunk, then sliced the meat off even with their teeth.

We watched them eat and smelled the cooking meat; and when you're hungry, I don't guess there's a better smell on earth than that of beef roasting over a mesquite-wood fire. Arliss got up and started toward them.

"I'm gonna git us some of that," he said.

"You better not tamper with them devils," I warned.

He didn't even look back. "I'm hongry," he said, and kept going.

He circled wide around the Apache whose ear he'd eaten and went to squat beside the Comanche.

"Gimme the loan of your knife," he said.

All he got was a blank stare, the Comanche not understanding. Arliss frowned with impatience. He pointed toward the roasting meat, then reached for the Comanche's knife. He lifted his voice, as if shouting would help the Comanche to understand.

"All I want is some meat," he explained.

For a wonder, the Comanche gave him the knife. Arliss stabbed the point of it into the biggest chunk of meat on the fire.

Instantly, the Comanche slapped the knife out of Arliss's hand, while all about him the squatted Apaches jerked to their feet, barking out sharp words of alarm. They glared down at Arliss, their eyes hot with anger.

Arliss glared back at them. "What's the matter?" he demanded. "Dang it! We're just as hongry as y'all are!"

The Comanche reached down and picked up the knife. The chunk of meat still hung to the blade. He held the meat out away from his body, staring at it like maybe it was poisoned. With a quick jerk of his wrist, he slung the meat off the blade of his knife, flinging it far out into the grass.

Arliss scowled. He stood looking hurt and mad while the Comanche wiped his knife blade across the leg of his breeches.

With the blade clean, the Comanche turned his back on the fire and lifted both hands—one holding the knife—high above his head. He looked up at the sky. He started talking in a singsong chant that reminded me of a brush-arbor preacher calling on the Almighty to save the souls of all us black-hearted sinners.

The chant went on for a good long spell. Listening to it gave me the creeps. But when it was finally over, the Indians all seemed to feel better and went back to eating.

35

That is, all but the Comanche. He handed the knife back to Arliss, then held Arliss's hand and showed him how to run the blade under a piece of meat instead of through it.

"I don't see what difference it makes," Arliss said.

I didn't, either. I didn't know then that no Comanche or Apache ever spears cooking meat. For some reason, that's considered an insult to their gods and is liable to bring down a mess of trouble on the tribe.

Arliss started toward us, careful to keep the meat balanced across the blade of the knife. With a grunt, the one-eared Apache rose suddenly to his feet. He stepped in front of Arliss and reached for the knife. Arliss pulled it back out of reach.

The Comanche barked at the Apache. The Apache turned on him, jabbering loud and hostile. It was plain that he didn't trust Arliss with a knife; and I guess he had some reason not to.

The Comanche heard him out, but didn't answer. He came and took the knifeload of hot meat from Arliss and brought it to us. He laid the meat on top of the boulder beside me and let Arliss use the knife to cut it into bite-sized pieces. Then he took the knife back and squatted down to make a careful study of us while we ate.

With my hands still tied, I couldn't feed myself, so Lisbeth did it for me. The meat was scorched on the outside, and half raw on the inside. It was all messed up with ashes and sand that gritted between my teeth. But it tasted good and was filling, and I began to feel almost grateful to the Comanche.

It bothered me, though, the way he kept studying us, watching our every move like we were some sort of curious varmints he'd never seen before. It made me mad, too.

I glared at him. "You needn't look at us like that," I said. "You're the wild one. Not us!"

He didn't answer. He just moved up closer, where I got a full load of his scent. It was rank and wild smelling, a strong mixture of armpit sweat and wood smoke and rancid grease and other odors I couldn't name.

He bent forward and stared straight into my eyes, looking long and hard, like a man trying to see through a smoky window glass to what's on the other side.

I stared back at him for as long as I could, then looked away.

My glance fell on the rawhide shield he wore on his left arm. It was round and dished, made of fire-hardened buffalo hide, with the hair on the inside. It was ornamented with a ring of grisly dried scalps dangling from its rim.

It wasn't the scalps that caught my interest, though. They just reminded me of all the people he'd murdered, and made me shudder. What took my eye was the strange designs painted on the face of the shield. It happened to be tilted at just the right angle for the firelight to show up a moon, some stars, snakes, turtles, and other figures, all laid out in such exact positions that they made a pattern I seemed to recognize.

An idea popped into my head. I looked up at the sky. It spread over us like a great blue star-studded bowl turned upside down. I studied the positions of the bigger stars for a moment, then looked back at the shield.

I'd been right. That thick-hided shield hadn't been made just to turn arrows and rifle balls. It mapped the sky in detail. I wondered if the Comanche could use it some way as a guide.

It shook me, coming to learn that a wild Indian was that smart. I couldn't have figured out and made a sky-map like that to save my skin; and I'd already learned enough to read three or four books all the way through. It gave me a new respect for the Comanche.

But this respect turned to hot resentment a few minutes later. We'd just finished up the last scrap of meat when suddenly, quick as a cat, the Comanche leaped on me and grabbed my feet. He had them tied together before I could even think to fight back.

I guess the surprise was just as big for Lisbeth and Arliss. Neither of them tried to run. They stood popeyed with scare till the Comanche had tied them up with extra strings that he carried in his belt.

When he finished, he just sort of heaped us up in a pile and went on back to the fire, where he dug out more meat and went to eating again.

I lay there, thinking hard. I couldn't figure out that Comanche. He didn't make sense. How come he'd treat us good one minute, then the next turn on us like a biting dog? I studied on it a good while, but I didn't come up with any answer that satisfied.

As the Indians got their fill of meat, they backed off from the fire. They squatted on their heels and smoked cigarettes of strong-scented tobacco rolled in clipped corn shucks. A couple loosened bowstrings that had evidently gotten wet when we crossed the river. They pushed the ends of the bows into the sand and let them stand with limp strings dangling near the fire, giving them a chance to dry out. They talked awhile, then, one by one, threw their cigarette butts into the fire and sprawled in the grass. They didn't bother to put a guard out, like white men would have done.

The fire died down. Things began to get quiet except for the usual night sounds—the call of the whippoorwills, the piping of the frogs around the water, the twittering of birds in the trees, the munching noises the horses made grazing on the grass.

Up on the hog-back ridge we had crossed, a wolf howled long and mournfully. Another one pitched in and helped out. They'd caught the scent of fresh meat, but I guessed sight of the fire had them stood off.

They tuned in on another big howl and beside me I felt a shiver run through Lisbeth. I felt sorry for her. I could remember when the howling of wolves used to make me shiver with scare.

Lisbeth said in a shaky whisper, "What're we going to do, Travis?"

I glanced toward the Indians. They all lay quiet. Maybe they weren't asleep yet, but best I could tell, they all had their eyes shut.

I whispered to Lisbeth. "Ease over close and get my knife out of my pocket. But take your time and be quiet about it."

I felt her shift around, slow and careful. Then her hand was in my pocket, fishing for my knife.

She got it, but couldn't thumb open the blade. I told her to hold it up to my mouth, and I bit the blade open. She cut the rawhide string binding my hands. Then I took the knife and cut us all free.

"Now, keep quiet," I warned. "Till we're dead certain they're all asleep."

We lay still and waited. I held the pocketknife open in my hand. When the time came, I wanted to be all set to cut the horse hobbles in a hurry.

The edge of a full moon began to inch up over the ridges. A "Comanche moon" was what the settlers called it, because it was during the time of a September full moon when the Comanches did most of their raiding. I guessed now it might get to be called an "Apache moon."

The fire died to a weak glow among the ashes. The wolves hushed their howling. A little later, I heard them snarling and growling at each other over the carcasses of the dead horse and the old longhorn cow who'd killed him. From the lower end of the valley came the booming hoot of a great horned owl. It was a ghostly sound and lonesome.

Listening to the owl set my mind to drifting. It slid way back in time to when I was just a knothead youngun, three or four years old, and pestering Mama every night to tell me what the owls were saying. And Mama came and stood right over me, her face all lighted up with fun, and I heard her say, like always, "Why, can't you tell? They're saying 'Who's cooking for yoo-oo? Who's cooking for *yoo*-all?' " So I laughed and snuggled down deeper into my corn-shuck bed, feeling warm and safe, knowing all along who was cooking for us.

Little Arliss

# Five

I GUESS in times of danger, a body's got senses
working for him that he doesn't even know about.
I didn't hear anything. I don't remember smelling or feeling
anything. And, dozed off like I was, I sure couldn't have
seen that Apache already crouched over and reaching for
Lisbeth. Yet suddenly the warning shot through me, so
strong and chilling that I lunged to my feet and had the
blade of my pocketknife buried in the back of the ugly devil
almost before my eyes popped open.

He went down under my knife blow with a howl of pain.
He landed on hands and knees, then pitched sideways
across Lisbeth, who screamed as she fought to get out from
under him. I went after him. I tripped over Little Arliss as
he started up with a cry of fear. I fell hard. But I was done
reaching for the black twisting shadow of the Apache, and
I had my knife into him a second time when I hit the
ground.

Then I was on him and all over him, kill-crazy with fear
and rage.

Behind me, I could hear the rest of the camp come
shouting to life, and while I struggled and stabbed and
slashed, I thought: *They'll get you. They'll kill you for this!*
But then I told myself: *Not before I get this one, they
won't!*

I was wrong on both counts.

I didn't get this one, because, during our desperate fight
there in the moonlight, he was lucky enough to grab my
knife hand and, in spite of how I'd cut him up, he still had
the strength to sling me head over heels through the air.

I landed in the sand and got a mouthful of it, and that's

40

where the others caught me and took over. The reason, I guess, that they didn't kill me for trying to kill him was that they could think up worse things to do.

They slapped me to the ground, where they kicked me. They yanked my boots from my feet and tore my pants off. They built up the fire and burnt my pants and boots, and then they jabbed glowing firebrands against my naked hide.

I'd lost my knife when I landed in the sand, but it wouldn't have done me any good now. They were too many for me. The grip of their hands on me was too tight. No matter how I bucked and pitched, I couldn't escape those firebrands. All I could do was grit my teeth against the horrible pain till I could smell the stench of my own flesh scorching. Then I'd lose control and scream and get to listen to the devils yelp with laughter every time I did.

How long this lasted, I don't know. Not long, I guess, else they'd have killed me. After a while, I blacked out, and when I came to, they were stringing me up to a drooping branch of one of the cottonwoods.

I hung face down, with my feet and hands tied together behind my back, with my weight all but pulling my arms out of socket at the shoulders. I hung so near the ground that my chest almost touched it. To add to my torment, one of the Apaches brought a big flat rock and laid it across my head, so that it kept my face pressed into the sand.

There I hung for the rest of the night, suffering more agony than it seems like a body could stand, suffering till I couldn't even think to wonder what had happened to Lisbeth and Little Arliss.

I suffered so much that every now and then I'd hear somebody groan, then come to realize that it was me. And every time I groaned, one of the Apaches would come and twist my ears or beat me with a stick or kick me again. I tried hard to stop groaning and couldn't. But after a while, I stopped anyhow, without trying—maybe because I was too far gone.

Out of the wild places, there are sounds to tell you when day is breaking, even if you're shut off from seeing the first faint light. In our country, the first sound is ordinarily the singing of the coyotes. Then comes the chatter and quarreling of the scissortail flycatchers. After that, it may be the fussing of the redbirds or the sharp clear call of a bob-white rooster quail in a hurry to get the day started. Or, if you happen to be in the right place, you can hear the heavy wing blows of wild turkeys threshing the tree branches as they quit their roosts, generally hitting the ground scattered, so that they've got to do a lot of yelping and stalking around to find each other again.

Such sounds are bound to have been all around me the next morning at daybreak. Yet, wrapped tight as I was in a black smothering coat of pain, I heard none of them.

Only one sound managed to get through to the part that was still me, and it had to have been the faintest, most faraway sound of them all. It was a clear, sweet, high-ringing bell note, as familiar a sound as I'd ever heard, yet one that in my tortured state I couldn't seem to place. It came through to me, over and over, almost as regular as my heartbeat, ringing out high, then fading, only to ring out again.

It fretted me, not being able to recognize that sound. I worried about it, certain that it was a thing within reach of my knowing, if only I could grab a hold on it. But my mind was like a red ant in a doodle-bug hole, clawing its way up the slant to the very edge of the trap, only to have the loose dry sand give way underfoot and let it slide back to the bottom. If only there was some way I could climb out of this trap of pain, I'd know in a second what that sound was.

Then, close beside me, I heard Little Arliss come alive, his voice shrill with excitement. "Listen! That's Savage Sam! He's a-trailin' us up!"

I came to my senses with a jolt. That was it. That's what my mind had been reaching for. The voice of Savage Sam!

Again, his faint, far-carrying trail cry came riding in on the still morning air. The sound of it raised a lump in my throat and put the sting of tears in my eyes.

There was a quick rush of footsteps toward me. The flat rock was shoved off my head. I twisted my stiff neck enough to recognize the figure of the tall Comanche as he cut me down from the cottonwood branch and dragged me over to the slanted boulder. He propped me against it, then left out in a run.

For a couple of seconds, the relief from hanging was so great that I almost fainted. Then the blood began to circulate in my legs and arms once more, and the pain of it made me dizzy and sick.

When my head cleared a little, I took a blurred look around. In the half-light of the coming day, I could see the Indians hustling about in a big hurry of excitement. One was bringing the horse herd in on the run, the hobbled horses goat-jumping awkwardly to keep up. Several Apaches ran out to meet the herd, where they were quick to free the hobbled horses. Others were busy picking up what loose gear they'd left lying around. Two scattered the ashes and charred wood left from last night's campfire, while another came running up with a dead bee-myrtle bush to sweep the place clean. Now, three came toward us, leading horses at a sweeping trot. One of them was the Comanche. He led the big bay I'd ridden the day before.

On reaching me, he jerked loose the knots in the string binding my feet. He yanked me to my feet, motioning for me to mount up.

How he expected me to climb astride that tall bay after what I'd been through the night before, I don't know. I couldn't even stand. I felt myself going down and twisted sideways so that I landed on my shoulder instead of my face. With a growl of anger, the Comanche grabbed me by the hair and one leg and flung me astride the horse. The bay's hair stung the galled places inside my bare legs.

While the Comanche bound me to the bay, I looked across to where two Apaches were tying Lisbeth and Little Arliss, each to a separate horse.

The sight of Arliss was enough to make me take a second look. He'd been painted all over, the same red as the skin of the Indians. Tied on his head was the tanned skin from a buffalo skull, with the curved black horns still attached. A foot of neck hide hung down over Arliss's back and shoulders like a black woolly cape.

A closer look at the Apache binding Lisbeth to her horse made my gorge rise. It was the broken-nosed one that I'd worked over with my pocketknife the night before. I'd laid his flesh open with enough deep cuts and slashes to have killed an ordinary man and it made me furious that he

*43*

hadn't died. But I could take some satisfaction in seeing how his wounds still seeped blood and how he crippled around. He was bad hurt, all right. I guessed he'd think twice before he laid a hand on Lisbeth again if I was anywhere in reach.

I wished I hadn't lost my pocketknife, though.

I said to Lisbeth and Arliss, "Why didn't y'all run last night? While I had my knife in that rascal?"

Lisbeth looked at me, then quickly away. "Wasn't nowhere to run to," she said.

"Anywhere would have done," I said. "Anywhere to get away from these red devils!"

Lisbeth didn't answer. She didn't look at me, either. She just sat there and kept her head turned away.

Then it came to me why she wouldn't look at me. I glanced down at myself and felt goose pimples of shame break out all over. I'd known it all along, of course, but the agony I'd suffered during the night had put it out of my mind. Now I saw that not only had I been painted as red as Little Arliss—I'd also been stripped just as naked!

Arliss said, "You wait till old Sam catches up! Then we'll git away!"

Mention of Sam took my mind off my nakedness. It was hard to believe that Sam was alive. I'd seen him chopped down by that tomahawk. I'd heard his screech of pain and seen the trail of blood he'd left as he'd gone wallowing and pitching down the slant of rocks.

Yet there was no doubt about it. He was not only still alive, he was on our trail. Or, anyhow, on the trail of Little Arliss. I'd heard him trailing Arliss often enough to recognize the pitch of his voice, which was different from when he was trailing a varmint. He was three or four miles behind, and not driving too fast, but coming on, sure and steady.

It was the constant ringing of Sam's voice that had the Indians disturbed. I could tell that by the way every now and then one of them would halt whatever he was doing to cock an ear in the direction of our back trail. I could tell by the quick uneasy glances they kept flinging over their shoulders, by the sharp questioning bark of their voices.

Maybe they didn't know what it was. Maybe they'd never

heard the singing voice of a trail hound before. Or maybe they knew exactly what it was and figured a band of armed white men was following that dog.

There was no way of knowing what they thought or didn't think, but one thing I could tell for certain: they knew *something* was on their trail, and they didn't like it and were bent on quitting that part of the country in a hurry.

Still looking away from me, Lisbeth spoke up, her voice desperate with hope. "You think anybody'll be with Sam?"

"Could be," I said, knowing the odds were all against it.

"Sure they is!" Arliss put in. "Betcha Sam's bringing Papa and a dozen others. First thing you know, there'll be dead Injuns scattered all over creation!"

The Apaches mounted up, the wounded Comanche grabbed me by the foot, and we were on the move again, traveling fast.

I rode with the brush scratching and clawing at my bare legs, wishing I could feel as confident as Little Arliss. I wished I could believe that the man who'd shot the Comanche had also seen Sam get cut down and had gone to him and carried him home and got Papa and all the other settlers they could round up and taken Sam back and put him on our trail and followed him all the rest of the day and on through the night. But I knew that was asking for a lot of luck.

Still, just knowing that Sam was on our trail gave me a lift. It was foolish, of course. Against the Indians, Sam would last about as long as it would take a whirlwind to suck up a dry corn shuck. Yet, for some reason, hope rode high inside me as we left the little half-moon valley, traveling north, climbing a rock rise, where the fast hoofbeats of the horses rang out sharp and loud in the still morning air.

At the top of the rise, two of the Apaches split off from the main bunch and swung right. Then my hopes withered.

It was plain those two meant to quarter in on our back trail and take a look at whatever was following us. They rode in the direction I figured would take them to the river at about where we'd crossed it the evening before. There, I guessed, they'd wait till Sam entered the water and started swimming across. Then they'd cut down on him with bows and arrows. And if they missed the first shots, they'd have plenty of time for seconds and thirds, what with Sam being out there in the open.

Thinking of Sam's getting killed with no chance to fight back made me heartsick. But since I couldn't help him, I tried to put my mind to problems I might could handle.

One of the main ones was how to keep from getting my head knocked off my shoulders. For by now, we had hit the bottom of the other side of the ridge, and here the country changed suddenly from sandstone to granite gravel and from short brush to thick stands of scrub blackjack and post oak. A heavy crop of acorns had the oak branches sagging. They hung at just the right height for the smaller ones to whip you blind or for the bigger ones to knock you clean off your horse if you weren't tied on.

I laid my head low against the bay's neck, then thought of Lisbeth and Little Arliss. They were mounted on loose horses now, and maybe wouldn't know how to protect themselves.

I lifted my head, searching. I spotted Lisbeth and Arliss riding close together. Their hands weren't tied, and both rode with a fistful of mane to help hold themselves on. That was good. But while Arliss had caught on to ride with his head down, like me and the Indians, Lisbeth hadn't. She was still trying to sit up straight, and having to duck and dodge every whichaway and still getting whipped over the head every time her horse ran under a tree. Any second now, she was liable to get slammed by a heavy tree branch that'd knock her off balance.

It gave me the cold chills to think what would happen if she ever slipped down to hang under her running horse. His hammering hind feet would crush her skull in a minute.

I yelled at her. "Lisbeth! Lay down on him. Like Little Arliss!"

She flung me a scared glance, then laid her head down beside her horse's neck. There, the drooping branches could still claw at her long hair and rake and tear at her dress. But hugged down close to her mount, she wasn't so likely to get knocked loose.

We rode a long time this way, then swept down into a broad open flat, where the timber thinned out, giving way to big granite boulders that stood high above the tall grass. The boulders were pink and orange, grayed over with age and weather. They looked old and solemn and quiet, like tombstones in a graveyard. One, nearly as big and a lot taller than our cabin, looked exactly like a monstrous Indian. He was squatted, with arms folded, wrapped to his chin in a blanket of pink-flowering morning-glory vine, and gazing out upon the rising sun.

I wasn't the only one to take notice of that rock. Before we'd reached it, the Comanche running beside me called out and pointed. The others looked and came suddenly alert. They swung their running horses wide around the Indian rock and kept glancing fearfully back over their shoulders long after we'd passed it.

I guess they were superstitious and looked on that big rock as some sort of heathen god. I know the sight of it prickled my scalp.

We rode past a little lake. Heavy live-oak timber stood back away from it. Between the timber and the water's edge bloomed the bluest flowers I ever saw, and the blue of them was reflected in the water.

We skirted the timber and went racing through the blue flowers, crushing them, and on through a tall stand of cat-tail grass, out of which red-wing blackbirds rose in clouds, screaming at us for disturbing them.

We left the lake and crossed a slight knoll. We went plunging down through a tall stand of yellow blooming sunflower whose stalks and leaves dragged fuzzy-rough and stinging against my bare skin. We crashed through a stand of willows that lined a wide sandy creek bed. A trickle of shallow water wound back and forth across the sand.

At one place, the sand was quick and sucked at the horses' feet, so that the animals had to pitch and lunge to fight free of bogging clear up to their bellies. Then we went out through more willows, entering an open, grassy flood plain that led alongside the creek.

We followed this creek for miles. Now and then the oak and pecan timber would squeeze in too close to the willows. When this happened, nearly always we could see open ground on the opposite side of the creek; so we'd cross over and keep going.

We rode till the sun got high and hot and set fire to my skin, some of which had already blistered from exposure the day before. We rode till flecks of white foam flew back from the horse's mouth to sting my eyes. We rode till the bay was in a lather of sweat, and the salt of that sweat stung my galled crotch.

I hoped Lisbeth and Little Arliss weren't suffering like I was. Lisbeth, of course, still had on her dress; and torn and tattered as it was by now, I figured it still had to be some protection. Arliss, he was used to the sun and wasn't likely to blister. Yet, riding naked and tied down hard to a sweat-lathered horse, he was bound to be rubbed raw, the same as me.

But if Arliss suffered, he wasn't letting out one whimper. He rode quiet, gripping a handful of horse mane, and glared black murder at the savages.

That was one thing I could tell for certain about Little Arliss—they hadn't taken the fight out of him yet!

I felt real proud of him.

My last drink of water had been the night before, and now thirst began to add to my misery. I kept hoping that at one of our many crossings of the sandy creek the Indians would stop for water, but they didn't. They never let up and finally swung away from the creek, heading northwest across more rocky, brush-covered hills.

We came to the San Saba River, with its clear sparkling waters purling over and around the rocks. It seemed like I just *had* to have a drink of that water; but I didn't get one, and neither did many of the horses. Some of the leaders got a few sips before the Indians came whooping up from behind, to send them splashing across the shallow stream with their ironshod hoofs popping loud against the flat rocks.

Then it was more hills, more brush, more rocky, deep-cut draws and canyons, with my suffering mounting steadily, so that after a time I rode in a daze of agony and hardly noticed when the ground began to smooth out and become open, rolling grassland.

Gradually, however, I did become aware of a mountain that stood alone, some distance away from the hills.

We rode toward it, and I noticed that one side was a gentle, brush-covered slope that rose higher and higher till suddenly it chopped square off, leaving a bare-rock cliff with different shades of coloring. We approached the sloping side.

We had reached the foot of the mountain, where the grass began to thin out and the brush to take over, when I heard the frightened wail of a rabbit.

An Apache riding just ahead of me heard it, too. He slid his running horse to a squat and waved his lance aloft. All the others swung their mounts toward him, leaving the loose horses to run on ahead. The Indians cut in front of me so quickly that my bay was forced to stop.

I heard the rabbit cry out again, then saw a cottontail dart from under a tickle-tongue bush and race off into the brush. At the same time, I saw the branches of the bush shake, then caught a glimpse of a snake slithering his way to the top. It was a prairie racer and in its mouth was a struggling half-grown cottontail.

The snake climbed quickly to the top of the bush. There it lay, with its whip body crooked around the thorny branches. If it heard or saw the horses and Indians gathering around, it paid them no mind, but went right to work swallowing its catch.

The cottontail was four times bigger around than the biggest part of the snake. But the snake seemed to know what it was doing. It had its mouth clamped shut over the nose of the cottontail, and I could see the widespread jaws spreading wider as the snake's neck muscles flattened and swelled, flattened and swelled, somehow always shoving those jaws forward to take in a bit more of the rabbit's nose.

I guess a snake's got the same right to eat as anybody else. I'd killed and eaten plenty of cottontails and never thought much about it. But, like most people, I always did hate snakes, and it was an ugly thing to sit and watch this one swallow down a helpless baby rabbit.

To me, it was strange, the way the Indians gathered round to watch, silent and intent, some even dismounting to come bend over the bush for a closer look.

I got to watching the Indians more than the snake. All yesterday and most of this morning, they'd kept on the run like they'd expected to be caught any minute. Then, at the cry of a captured animal, they'd stopped to waste all this time watching the rabbit get swallowed by a snake—as curious about it as Little Arliss might have been. It didn't make sense.

But then, what about an Indian did make sense? Why would they raid for horses, then run them so hard and long that half of them would end up wind-broken and worthless? Why capture us, then mistreat us till we were liable to die on their hands before they ever got to wherever they meant to take us?

There was no answer to that one. So I just sat there on the bay horse, dizzy with thirst and the pain of the sun blazing down on my fire burns, which were now beginning to fester and seep clear water.

I looked up the brushy slope, searching for Lisbeth and Little Arliss. The horses had scattered. Some were grazing, but most of them stood spraddle-legged with their heads down, trying to get back their wind. I saw Lisbeth not too far away, and Little Arliss a couple of hundred yards off, both still tied to their horses and looking toward us, both wondering, I guess, at what was going on.

We waited there for twenty, maybe thirty minutes, watching the snake stretch himself wider and wider and squeezing the rabbit down smaller and smaller as he swallowed it. Finally, the hind feet of the rabbit disappeared. The snake's muscles quit working for a moment and the snake lay still.

That's when several of the watching Indians straightened and grunted, sounding like they were satisfied with the show. Then, grinning, the one-eared Apache drew his tomahawk from his belt. With a quick flashing stroke, he chopped the snake's head clean off; and they all whooped with laughter as the rest of the snake's body whipped high into the air, then spilled down out of the bush onto the ground. The headless snake was still writhing and twisting and slinging spurts of blood around when the Indians turned to mount up and ride toward the top of the mountain.

*Apache*

# Six

THE highest part of the mountain was at the brink of the cliff, and that's where we stopped. Here the riders rounded up the loose horses and held them, bunched tight against the edge, while they all gazed out across the country beyond. It was a vast expanse of rolling grassland, broken in only a few places by dark, straggling lines of timber which marked the watercourses. It stretched on and on toward the west, farther than a body could believe, reaching so far out that it finally faded to nothing in the misty blue haze of distance.

This, I knew, was the edge of the South Plains, a lower section of *El Llano Estacado,* as the Spanish called that great wilderness of grass that some said reached north from the Rio Grande clear into Canada. I'd heard tell of it, but never seen it before; and in spite of how dazed I was with hurts and doubts and fears, my first glimpse of all that wide spread of emptiness struck me a solid jolt.

Once Papa had tried to tell me and Little Arliss what the ocean looked like, but this was the first time I ever got a clear picture of what he was talking about.

I'd been told that white men had crossed this country,

but only the Indians knew it; and now I wondered how even they could know it all. It was just so big!

I looked to see what they searched for. A mile out, I located a band of antelope. Some were grazing and some were lying down. All seemed contented and willing to take things easy, except for four sentinels that stood away from the herd a piece, each guarding a different side. The sentinels stood stock-still and high-headed, alert to give warning of any danger.

Farther out, so far that the rising heat waves made everything wavery, I saw lumps of black against the green of the grass. I took these to be buffalo, but couldn't know for sure.

And overhead, high against a few cotton-white puffballs of clouds, a couple of eagles wheeled slowly on widespread wings, screaming at regular intervals.

Those were the only living creatures I could see. They must have been all the Indians could see, too, for finally one of them grunted, and they all turned to search our back trail.

They looked it over just as closely, but not for so long. Then one reached into a buckskin bag hanging to his belt and drew out a little square mirror of polished steel. He squinted up at the sun. He swung his horse around to face a different direction, then held up the mirror. With quick twists of his wrists, he flicked the face of the mirror back and forth.

Where I sat my horse, watching, I was almost facing the mirror; and once, a blaze of reflected sunlight caught me full in the eyes, nearly blinding me.

After that, I turned and looked along our back trail, like the Indians; and before long, I saw a quick wink of light from some high place far back in the wooded hills. Then another and another.

There were some sharp, barking words among the Indians. It came to me then what was going on. This bunch was swapping signals with other Indians, probably the two who had gone to ambush Sam.

Evidently, the Indians were satisfied with what they'd learned. They all relaxed. The herders opened up and let the loose horses move away from the edge of the cliff.

They got behind them and drove them back down the side of the mountain. At the bottom, we swung west, then north past the face of the cliff, traveling at a walk, which gave the horses time to nip at the grass clumps as we moved along.

An hour later, the two Apaches who had left at daylight overtook us. They came galloping up on lathered mounts, driving six more horses ahead of them. All stopped then to hold a big jabbering powwow.

I looked the new horses over. It was a relief to note that they all wore the same brand, a Circle Seven on the right hip. That meant that they had been stolen from Charlie Severs, who raised horses along the Llano. They hadn't been taken from Papa or any of the other Salt Licks settlers who might be on our trail now.

The newcomers acted braggy about something. They talked big and waved their lances and rifles about in the air. When the others didn't appear too happy about what they had to say, one of the newcomers got mad. He stabbed his lance into the ground. He glared around at the others, daring anybody to pick up the quarrel.

Nobody did, but I noticed that the main bunch seemed uneasy about something; and when we moved on, it was at a fast pace again. It wasn't a dead run, like before, but it was at a pretty smart clip.

I rode with the trotting Comanche holding to my foot. I numbed myself the best I could against the burning pain of my outside body and the fearful dread that lay cold and heavy on my inside.

I kept asking myself, *Did they get Sam?* I didn't see how they could have missed if they'd gone back after him. And what with the way they'd all got so excited when they heard his voice, that's bound to have been what they went for.

Still, there were those extra horses they'd brought in. Could they have run onto the horses and forgotten Sam? Or did they kill Sam first and then pick up the horses? I could tell myself that whether they'd killed Sam or not wasn't likely to make much difference in what happened to us. Yet, it seemed like I just had to know, and my mind kept gnawing at it like a dog worrying an old bone.

A gentle breeze started pulling in from the south, cooling my sunburned back and setting the tall grass to nodding and whispering. The breeze grew stronger. It lifted and set streaming the manes and tails of the horses. It raced across the grass in great shimmering waves, and the whispering of the grass grew louder. By noon, the wind drove with a force that all but flattened the grass to the ground and had it booming like far-off thunder.

I looked to the north, expecting to see the makings of a big rainstorm. All I could see, though, was the glint and sparkle of the hot sunlight on the tossing grass. If there was a rain cloud building up, it had to be clear off the rim of the earth.

We didn't see any buffalo for a while, but their trails were everywhere. Some trails were worn so deep and narrow that I could see where the grass-swelled bellies of the huge animals had scraped both sides of the trail, dragging loose little wads of hair that still stuck to the dirt walls. Mostly, we followed one buffalo trail or another; but if we happened to be crossing them and came to a deep one, the horses all had to jump it.

I guess it was the whoop and roar of the wind that made our meeting with the two white men such a big surprise for both parties.

We came jog-trotting down off the high prairie into a cut-bank draw. The draw led into a wide-open flat that I could see just beyond. The high dirt banks shut off the wind for a moment, and I remember feeling the touch of relief you always notice when you first take cover from a high wind. Then we were out in the open again and there, gathered around a water hole, was a band of some thirty mares with colts, along with a couple of stud horses.

The studs were fighting. They were reared up and squealing, chopping at each other with their forefeet, trying to grab neck holds with their bared teeth.

Just beyond, in the shade of a cottonwood, squatted a couple of white men. They sat on their spurs, holding the bridle reins of their saddled mounts while they watched the studs fight. One was an old man dressed in buckskins and wearing his hair long under a wide-brimmed black hat.

54

The other was maybe twenty-five or -six, and wore the usual cowhand garb.

Suddenly the white men saw us. They came to their feet with shouts of alarm, while the mounted Apaches cut loose with whoops and screeches. All this racket stampeded the mares and colts, so that they wheeled away from the water, snorting and lunging. They scattered and got in the way of the Indians and gave the white men time to mount up.

"Cut for the dugout!" I heard the old man yell.

Then all of us—white men, mounted Indians, our horses, and the whole band of mares, colts, and studs—took out down the draw in a wild run.

The two white men had six-shooters and knew how to use them, judging by the number of horses they shot from under the Apaches.

But hitting an Apache was something else. All the white men had to shoot at was a part of one leg hooked across the back of a horse and a shield clamped against the horse's neck. The rest hung out of sight on the off side.

At first, I couldn't see how those red devils could cling to a running horse like that. Then I noted that they had tied loops in their horses' manes and had their shield arms run through the loops. Hanging there, using their mounts' bodies for protection, they shot from under the necks of the horses. Some used bows and arrows. Most of them fired repeater rifles. One or two made short throws with their feathered lances.

The only real chance the white men ever had was when they knocked a rider's horse down. Then all they'd get was one quick running shot before the Indian had bounded to the back of another horse and slipped down off its side, where the horse's body would protect him.

The Apaches got the young man first. I saw him throw up his hands and slip from the saddle. He hit the ground, and the frightened horses snorted and lunged aside, trying to keep from stepping on him; but they were too hard pressed from behind. Some trampled on him, anyhow.

Then we were past, and I looked ahead in time to see the old man's horse stumble and start going down. But the old man was nimble as any Indian; he quit his saddle and hit the ground running and he ran with a speed that had his long gray hair streaming backward from under his hat.

I saw then the place he was making for: the dark hole of a dugout set in the side of a sharp slope near some live oak trees. Feathered arrows stabbed the ground around his racing feet and rifle balls kicked up spurts of dust beyond. But nothing touched him; and for a second, I thought he was going to make it.

Then a ball took him in the back, seeming to lift him clear off his feet before tumbling him to the ground. Instantly, he rolled over, got to his hands and knees, and shot a horse from under another Apache.

He was still snapping an empty six-shooter in their faces when the yelping pack leaped from their horses to swarm over him.

My Comanche bounded ahead to clutch the running bay by one ear and his underjaw, dragging him to a stop beside the close-packed Indians. The group parted, and I saw the old man now lying flat on his back, with a lance thrust through his side, pinning him to the ground.

Arliss's one-eared Apache held the lance. A moon-faced, bandy-legged Indian had a grip on the old man's long hair. Both held drawn knives and argued furiously. Others joined in the argument.

Finally, Gotch Ear snatched his lance from the old man's body. He grabbed up the black hat that lay on the ground close by and clapped it on his head. He shoved his way roughly through the group and walked off, his face a thunder cloud of anger. It was plain he'd lost the argument over the old man's scalp.

I'd sat watching, petrified with horror, and got a bigger shock when I saw the old man's eyelids flutter open. He looked straight up at me. He gasped. His body jerked, then slowly flattened and lay quiet. His eyes were still open and still staring up at me; but the light had gone out of them. He wasn't seeing me anymore.

Bandy Legs scalped him then and waved the scalp aloft, yelping his pleasure.

The Indians were real proud of what they'd done. They strutted and they boasted and they bragged. They robbed the dead men of their knives, six-shooters, and rifles and argued over who was to get which. They held an even hotter argument over who the scalp of the young man belonged to. They rounded up the scattered mares and colts, pointing out special animals to admire. They circled the milling band of horses and gloated at the big haul they'd made.

I'd heard tell that Plains Indians prized stolen horses above anything else, and it was easy to see that when this bunch finally reached camp—wherever that was—they figured to make a real showing.

All their boasting and bragging sickened me. I looked away from it toward the skimpy camp of the white men. Their shelter they'd made by digging a hole back into a dirt bank. They'd roofed the hole over with logs, then piled dirt on top of the logs. They'd raised a garden there on that dirt roof, packing water to it, I guess, from the creek below. Some okra and tomato plants were still alive. I could see the red of several ripe tomatoes among the green of the sprawling vines.

Near the dugout door was the ash pile of a still smouldering campfire. It was ringed with flat rocks and on the rocks sat a fire-blackened coffee pot and a big Dutch oven.

The sign was easy to read. The old man and the young one had come to raise horses on free grass. They'd brought along a bunch of mares and a couple of studs. They'd aimed to rough it out here in the wilds, gambling on staying alive till they could build up a horse herd worth trailing to New Orleans or maybe to California—just wherever they figured on horses bringing the best price. It was a way of raising a good stake of cash money for whatever they hoped to do later on down the line.

A lot of young men took that gamble in those days. Once me and Papa had talked some about giving it a whirl. But Mama, she'd put her foot down, hard; and for every man we could mention who had cleaned up a pot of money that way, she could name three who'd lost both their horses and their hair.

At the time, I'd been mighty disappointed and had looked on Mama's arguments as the same brand of scare talk you could generally expect of womenfolks. Now, I could see Mama'd had some room to argue.

In the excitement, I hadn't missed my Comanche. Suddenly, he appeared in the doorway of the dugout, packing a roll of blankets and a couple of hackamores of braided horsehair. This loot he carried to my horse, Blue. He hung the hackamores over the saddle horn and tied the blankets on back of the cantle. Then he came toward me, wearing a puzzled frown on his paint-streaked face as he studied a small object in his hand.

I didn't pay him much mind. I was too sick with hurt and shock to care what he had found. But when he held it up to me, I looked.

It was a tintype picture of a young woman. She was about twenty years old. She wore the stiff, scared smile that most people wear when they're getting their pictures struck. But she was a pretty woman, with long blond hair like Lisbeth's. She didn't look like Lisbeth, yet there was something about her eyes and the curve of her lips that gave you the same warm feeling. You could tell at a glance that she was the sort a young man would love—wanting her bad enough to take most any sort of gamble to provide her with a nice home and the pretty things a woman generally hopes for.

The Comanche withdrew the picture and peered up at me like he wanted the answer to some question on his mind. I didn't know what the question was, but I boiled with plenty of hot answers.

"You stinking, murdering devils!" I railed at him. "You kill her man, then expect me to tell you who she is and where she is and how you can get your filthy hands on her!"

I was all wound up to tell him more, but got stopped by a loud commotion.

It was Gotch Ear, black hat and all, mounted on one of the stud horses. The stud was reared high, pawing the air with his forefeet. At the same time, he was running backward on his hind feet and squealing his rage.

Maybe I was wrong, but the thought hit me that in mounting that stud, Gotch Ear was making a strong bid for glory. He'd been jeered at for losing an ear to Little Arliss. The Comanche had stood him off with a lance when he tried to get revenge. Then he'd laid claim to the long-haired scalp of the old man, but the others had let Bandy Legs have it. Now, he aimed to wipe out the shame of all this with a show-off ride on a bad horse.

Well, it was a ride to watch and remember. The stud was reared so high it looked like he was bound to topple over. Then he dropped back to the ground and started whirling in a tight circle. He whirled with a speed hard to believe. He had his neck bowed, his ears laid back, and his teeth bared. He was doing his savage best to bite that Apache's leg clear in two. But Gotch Ear rode with his leg always just a little out of reach.

The stud was big and stout and a mean fighter. He had plenty of other tricks in his bag. Quick as lightning, he whipped his head around for a bite at the other leg. This time, he came so close that he left tooth marks on Gotch Ear's leg, which set all the watching Apaches to yelping.

Missing out on that bite, the stud reared again. When he came down this time, it was to tuck his tail and bog his head and take out across the draw, pitching and bawling the wildest I ever saw.

That Gotch Ear was a rider. All he had to hold onto was a fistful of mane and a sense of balance. All he rode was a little patch of that stud's back no bigger than the palm of your hand. His legs and one free arm, they were loose as rags. They flew out in all directions. Just now and then one of them swung back to touch the stud's neck or shoulder or maybe his ribs before flinging out into the air again.

And all the time, the bawling stud was putting everything he had into unloading that Indian. He pitched forward, sideways, and in circles. He crawfished. He rolled his belly up to the sun. And every time he landed, it was with all four legs as stiff as crowbars and all four feet planted close together—hitting the ground so hard, you could have stood a quarter of a mile off and heard the *whoomp* of the air in his belly.

Yet not once did I see daylight between Gotch Ear's rump and that little patch of back hide it seemed glued to. Gotch Ear had that stud horse rode. He had him rode right down to a whisper—if it hadn't been for his black hat.

I guess he'd never worn a hat before. He didn't seem to

know the importance of pulling one down to a tight set before mounting a bad horse.

Now the hat loosened and with every leap the stud made, it inched forward a little, till finally it was clear down on Gotch Ear's nose, shutting off his vision.

That's when Gotch Ear made his big mistake. He reached to straighten his hat and lost his balance.

The stud threw him so high I saw him swap ends in the air above the highest branches of a stooping mesquite that stood between us.

He landed on his feet, running, but he was still lucky that mesquite stood so close by. For the stud had wheeled and was after him with a fire in his eyes that said he aimed to kill an Indian.

I hoped he caught him.

He nearly did, too. His breath was warming the seat of Gotch Ear's breechclout when that Apache leaped halfway up the trunk of the stooping mesquite and went scrambling toward a higher perch.

There he squatted, barely out of reach of the screaming stud, who reared high, chopping loose great chunks of bark from the tree trunk with flailing hoofs, biting off smaller branches in his savage attempt to get at the man who'd tried to ride him. There Gotch Ear squatted, forced to listen to the delighted yelps and jeers of his companions, who took their time and hoorawed him to their hearts' content. And in both cases, he was helpless to do more than glare around with hate and defiance.

Satisfied at last with the fun they'd had, the others moved in on the stud. They whipped him and goaded him with lance points until they finally drove him away.

Even after they'd done so, Gotch Ear squatted there in the mesquite a good long while before he climbed down. He wasn't scared. He was just mad—and pouting.

Here he'd gone and made a try to prove himself as much a man as any of the others, and what had come of it? He'd lost everything—his pride, his dignity, the respect he'd hoped to win.

All he had left was his big black hat.

*Apache*

# Seven

LIKE before, when we got around to leaving out, it was in a high run. We swept up out of the draw onto higher ground and went charging across the open prairie like there wasn't a minute to lose.

We jumped a small band of antelope. They went racing off at an angle, their white-tail flags lifted high, traveling at a far greater speed than ours. We skirted a mile-wide prairie-dog town, where thousands of the plump little gray-yellow dogs sat over their holes and barked at us in squeaky voices, quick to drop back into the ground when we came too close.

Living among the dogs were tiny brown owls with big heads and great white circles around their eyes. Alarmed by our passing, they skipped and hopped from one hole to another.

We stampeded several small bunches of buffalo, then one great herd that numbered in the thousands. The pounding hoofs of the shaggy beasts shook the earth as they lumbered across the prairie, leaving in their wake a boil of dust and trash that the whooping wind whipped back into our faces.

An hour of this sort of travel, and the horse herd began to string out, the tougher and faster animals taking the lead. Among the stragglers was old Jumper; and this time, I could tell, he wasn't throwing off. The Indians shouted at him. They lashed him cruelly. They jabbed his rump with their lances till the blood came and Jumper brayed with the pain of it. Still, he kept falling further behind.

All mules are born tough, and Jumper was one of the toughest. Yet, a mule's not built for speed; and Jumper was old—too old to stand up to the relentless pace set by the Indians. He'd just about gone his limit, and no amount of mistreatment was going to make him keep up much longer.

The Apaches kept after him, though, and got four or five more miles out of him before we dropped down into a wide flat draw that wound in from the west.

There was runoff water here, left from the last rains. It stood in a number of potholes strung out along the draw. White-flowering cacanilla and scattered bunches of quick-growth mesquite stood among the tall sunflowers.

Thirsty horses plunged into the potholes, taking us captives with them. The horses drank and churned up the water with pawing hoofs, drank some more, then straggled out, looking for graze.

But Jumper didn't drink. Goaded by the Indians, he'd managed to stumble along until he was within sight of the water. But the second they let up on him, he'd stopped and stood there among the trampled sunflowers, with his head down and his shoulders hunched, shivering all over.

The Indians came and bellied down for a drink, again sucking up the water through wadded-grass strainers.

Gotch Ear was the first to rise. He hadn't had the sense to shove his black hat to the back of his head while he drank. Now, water spilled down from its brim and the wind blew it into his face. All he did about it, though, was to give his head a quick shake, like a wet dog, slinging water in all directions as he walked away.

I paid him no more mind, for now the Comanche rose from the water and came toward me. I hoped desperately that he aimed to turn me loose for a drink. I hadn't had water since the night before. All morning, I'd been spitting cotton, till finally I'd gotten too dry for even that. Now, my throat was on fire, and it seemed like if I didn't get water soon, I'd go crazy.

The Comanche came on and had just started working the

knots loose at my feet when I heard Little Arliss scream. I looked toward where he sat tied to his drinking horse and saw him staring in horror at some sight I hadn't yet seen.

"They've kilt him!" he cried out. "Travis! They've went and kilt old Jumper!"

I looked around. Jumper still stood, head down and trembling, the same as before; only, now, his life's blood gushed out through a slit across his gullet. Beside him, Gotch Ear wiped a bloody knife blade clean across the old mule's rump.

Jumper tried to bray, but all that came out was a strangled cough and a big gout of blood. The cough shook him. His legs buckled and he went down.

Arliss was suddenly wild with rage. He cut loose with a stream of words so foul you wouldn't believe a boy his age could know them. He screamed at Gotch Ear, and while he swore, he hammered frantically at his horse's back with balled-up fists, scaring the horse into lunging up out of the water hole. The animal shied around, snorting and whistling.

"Arliss!" I shouted at him. "You hush that cussing! You hear me?"

I was scared of the anger I could see mounting in Gotch Ear's face as he listened to Little Arliss's ranting and raving. Gotch Ear didn't have to understand the words to know he was being insulted. Now, he jabbed his knife into his belt and went striding through the sunflowers toward Little Arliss. His black eyes glittered with such evil intent that I panicked.

"Arliss!" I screamed. "You listen to me, now. You hush up that cussing!"

For once, Arliss listened. Or, more likely, he'd just reached a breaking point. Anyhow, he hushed suddenly; his face crumpled, and he tucked his chin and burst into tears, crying so hard that he didn't even fight back when Gotch Ear came and jerked loose the knots binding him to the horse.

Gotch Ear yanked him off the horse by one leg and slung him fifteen feet through the air. Arliss landed in one of the shallow potholes with a splash.

Gotch Ear stood back, grinning like he'd done something special.

The Comanche hauled me down off the bay and got mad all over again because I couldn't stand. He grabbed me by the hair. He dragged me to the water and dropped me face down in it. Now I could drink, all right, but I might have drowned afterward, trying to back uphill with my hands tied behind me, if the weeping Arliss hadn't waded out in time to give me a hand.

Arliss clung to me, shaking with sobs. He kept saying over and over, "They went and kilt old Jumper, Travis! They went and kilt old Jumper!"

Like he thought I could do something about it.

"Well, crying won't help," I told him.

I'd never seen Arliss like this before. I'd seen him cry plenty of times—mostly when he was fighting mad about something. But I'd never seen him break down and sob his heart out, like he was doing now. And it was the first time I could ever remember his calling me for comfort.

That shook me almost worse than seeing old Jumper killed.

With my burning thirst dulled a little, I looked around for shade. I saw a small dark patch under a bunch-topped mesquite. I staggered to my feet and had a dizzy spell. My ears roared; the ground rocked under me. I waited till the spell passed, then went stumbling toward the mesquite, with the weeping Arliss still clinging to me.

I flopped down in the shade. Lisbeth came toward us with tears running down her cheeks. She squatted beside Arliss and put her arms around him. She loved him up and tried to comfort him like Mama would have done. She tore a rag from her petticoat and went and soaked it in the water and came back and washed Arliss's face.

As she turned to wash me, she glanced toward the Indians. She gasped and looked quickly away. She said in a horrified voice, "Don't look now, Travis!"

So, naturally, I looked—and saw the Indians cutting chunks of meat from Jumper's rump.

My rage against the Indians rose to a pitch that nearly drove me wild.

I thought back over all the years we'd had Jumper. I remembered the many times he'd made me so mad that I'd wanted to kill him myself—for wheeling and kicking; for balking when he thought a load was too heavy; for always hunting something to take a scare at, so he'd have an excuse for running away and tearing up a cart or plow or a set of harness; for deciding for himself when it was time to quit work, sometimes taking out right in the middle of the field and heading for the cabin.

Yet, for all the years we'd had him, old Jumper had done the heavy work around our place. He'd pulled our plows. He'd hauled in our crops. He'd dragged up building logs. He'd packed in the wild meat we shot. When we cleared new ground or gathered slab rocks for fence building, it had been old Jumper's strength and sweat that had gone into moving those drag-sled loads of rock.

On top of all that, Jumper was *our* mule, which, I guess, was the main thing. Generally speaking, whatever thing belongs to you, whether it happens to be good or bad, seems to become a part of you. So that when you see it destroyed —especially in the cruel way we saw old Jumper destroyed —well, it's just natural for the hurt to go deeper.

There for a little bit, I was right on the edge of throwing in with Arliss and crying my eyes out—all on account of a cantankerous, butt-head mule.

The Indians gathered dead wood and built a fire around the trunk of a squat green mesquite. They brought long strips of backstrap and rump meat, cut from Jumper's carcass. They hung the strips in the forks of the mesquite and across the lower branches, where the heat of the fire could roast them.

They gutted the old mule and cut off a four- or five-foot section of the main gut. They tied up one end of it, making it into a sack. They filled this sack with water, then tied up the other end. They carried it to one of the saddled horses and hung it across the saddle and tied it down, so it wouldn't slip off. Then they went back and squatted around the fire and started eating the ends off the meat strips which hung closer to the fire and cooked faster than the rest.

They'd take their knives and lift the ends of the strips out away from the fire and blow on them till they could bite into the meat. Then they'd slice off the bite and let the rest of the strip swing back to hang over the fire and cook a while longer.

When a strip of meat had cooked enough to suit them, they'd lift it from the fire-blackened branch it hung on and hang it higher. When four or five of these strips had hung away from the fire long enough to cool, they'd tie them into a bundle and go catch a saddled horse and tie the bundle to the saddle.

After a while, the Comanche brought a strip of meat and handed it to Lisbeth and gave her his knife to cut it with. Then he squatted down on his hunkers to make another careful examination of us. I couldn't tell if he was the only one who cared whether we got anything to eat, or if he was just curious and looking for an excuse to study us some more.

Arliss had nearly stopped crying, but sight of that meat broke him down again.

"I can't eat none of old Jumper," he wailed.

"Eat it," I told him. "The way it's been, no telling when you'll eat again."

"But I can't," he sobbed. "What'd old Jumper think? Us eatin' him?"

"Jumper won't care," Lisbeth said. "He knows you got to eat." She cut him off a chunk. "Anybody can eat an Indian's ear can eat mule meat!"

Arliss held the meat and stared down at it and dripped tears all over it. Then he looked up at me.

"You think old Jumper won't mind?" he asked.

"He won't mind," I said.

So Arliss bit into the meat, and once started, ate it all and a couple more pieces. Which was better than I did. I couldn't hardly choke it down to save my life, and I noticed Lisbeth didn't have much better luck.

After all our wild rush to get to where we were, the Indians now lazed around camp like they had all the time in the world. Some kept right on eating, stopping now and then to go for a drink of water or to slice fresh strips of meat from old Jumper's carcass. Some sprawled for a snooze in the skimpy shade of the mesquites. Some just sat around smoking and talking.

This gave the horses a chance to graze and rest up. It gave little Arliss time to cry himself to sleep. And it gave Lisbeth a chance to help me down to water for another drink.

After that, I lay still and let her wash the dirt and stinging salt sweat from my fire- and sunburned body. Then she went to the fire and lifted down a cooled strip of meat. None of the Indians raised any fuss, and she brought it and began rubbing it gently into my burns.

"There's not much grease in it," she said, "but it was the fattest piece I could find."

"It'll help," I said. "Old Jumper wasn't the sort of mule to put on much fat."

That was about all that was said between us the whole time we were there; after all, what else was there to say?

Along in the shank of the evening, after the sun had sunk past the point of being so scorching hot, the Indians came and tied us back on our horses.

The Comanche flung me astride the bay; and it took all I had to keep from screaming when my raw skin touched the prickly, sweat-salted hairs of the horse's back. It was like being set astraddle of a coal of fire.

Lisbeth, I could tell, was plenty miserable, too, but she didn't cry out. Arliss, tougher than either of us, didn't seem to mind at all. My big worry about him was that he didn't fight back. He just sat on his horse with his head bent and his eyes shut, like he was asleep.

"Arliss," I called to him. "You keep awake and hold on. You slip down under the belly of that horse, and he'll scatter your brains all over the ground!"

Arliss paid me no mind.

Lisbeth touched heels to her horse and moved him up beside Little Arliss.

"Wake up, Arliss," she said.

Arliss paid her no mind, either.

Lisbeth reached out and got hold of one horn of Arliss's buffalo headdress. She used it to shake his head.

Arliss came alive then. He grabbed her wrist and held it.

"Whatta you shaking me around for?" he complained. "I ain't done nothing."

"Just trying to keep you awake," Lisbeth said.

"Well, I ain't sleeping," he said. "I'm just setting here, thinking. About how they went and kilt old Jumper. I'm aiming to make somebody pay for that!"

The Indians had spread out and rounded up the grazing horses, and now we headed west in a jog trot. We followed the winding watercourse, now and then cutting across some of its widest crooks.

The wild and worrisome wind that had tugged at us for so long had settled down to a gentle, cooling breeze. And what with my thirst gone and a little meat inside me, I was able to take my mind off my hurting and put it back to figuring out a plan of escape. There *had* to be some way of getting us out of the fix we were in.

I thought hard, but couldn't seem to come up with anything better than the plan I'd worked out the night before. I still felt that if Broken Nose hadn't come for Lisbeth when he did, that plan might have worked. It still looked like our best bet, if we could ever catch the Indians off guard.

The big trouble now was the loss of my knife. Without it, we'd have to steal horses that weren't hobbled, and that wouldn't be easy. I was a pretty high jumper when I put myself to it. With luck, I just might manage to sneak up on a horse and leap astride, like the Indians did. But that wouldn't work for Lisbeth and Little Arliss.

I tried to think up ways to steal a knife that Lisbeth might keep hidden inside her dress. Just then, one of the Apaches cut loose with a shout, and I felt the Comanche's grip tighten on my leg. I started up out of my thinking and took a quick look around.

At first, all I saw was mounted Indians racing back and forth behind the herd, whooping and lashing the horses, goading them into a run. The Comanche spanked my bay and he leaped forward to join the others. Then I looked further out and saw a sight that kicked my heart up into my throat.

It was *soldiers!*

There were fifteen or twenty of them. They were still half a mile off, but it was easy to tell they were United States cavalrymen by the blue of their uniforms, by the way they rode in double-rank file.

68

I heard the brassy blare of a bugle. I saw the glint of sunlight on the officer's saber blade, lifted high for the signal to charge.

I rode with the blood pounding in my eardrums. I rode with my hopes in as wild a stampede as the spooked horses racing along beside me. I watched the soldiers come charging down upon us, gaining fast, dead certain in my own mind that our freedom was just a few minutes off.

Once those troopers hit us, I guessed these bloodthirsty devils would learn what real fighting was all about. United States soldiers were *trained* to kill Indians. They'd cut this bunch to pieces in no time.

Maybe that's what my Comanche thought, too. Or maybe, like some of the horses, he'd traveled too fast for too long and was beginning to wear down. Anyhow, I felt his grip leave my foot and looked around to see him leap high. He landed back of me astride the bay and went to whacking his lance across the big horse's rump, trying to get more speed out of him.

By now, the stolen horses were stretched out, thundering over the turf at a pace that the colts and weaker horses couldn't hold. One by one, these began to fall behind, and the screeching Indians let them. They had no time now for whipping up the stragglers. The soldiers, evidently mounted on fresh horses, were gaining too fast.

The bay I rode was a big rangy horse with plenty of bottom. Even with a rider, he could have held his own with most horses in the bunch. But under the double load he packed now—better than three hundred pounds—he didn't stand a chance. In spite of the beating the Comanche gave him, he began to fall behind.

The guns of the troopers opened on us. Ahead of me a horse turned a somersault; but his rider didn't turn with him. He hit the ground, still on his feet. A moment later, he had leaped out onto the back of a passing horse.

We tore into another stand of mesquite and tall sunflowers. The mesquites were scrubby, just high enough for their thorny branches to whip my face. I bent low to the left and felt the Comanche lean down on the right. A second later, I learned that it wasn't just to shed the brush that he'd bent down. It was to cut my right foot free of its bind-

69

ings. Suddenly, he straightened and gave me a hard shove.

I hit the ground rolling, so that it was no real hurt that made me lie there in the sunflowers dead still for a long moment. It was just the shock and surprise at being free.

Then I leaped to my feet, aware of the pound of horses' hoofs charging past, knowing it was the soldiers by the clank and rattle of their gear. I went racing toward them through the mesquites and sunflowers, screaming at the top of my voice, "Kill 'em! Kill 'em!"

I broke out into the clear, still screaming, as the tail end of the column swept past.

Then I jerked up short. Barely in time, I realized that the last trooper had swung his rifle around and was taking aim at me!

I yelled and flung myself to the ground. The rifle crashed. A spindly mesquite sprout toppled and fell across me. The stub that was left stood just back of where I'd stood an instant before.

I lunged to my feet, scared and mad. I ran out to where I could see the troops tearing along after the Indians. I shook my fist at the one who had fired at me.

"You crazy fool!" I shouted after him. "Can't you see I'm white?"

The words had barely left my mouth when it came to me that I was the fool, not him. How could he know I wasn't an Indian? Me, stark naked and painted up like one.

All of a sudden, I went chasing after the soldiers and the fleeing Indians. I went racing through the tall grass, dragging a strip of rawhide still tied to one ankle. It was hard to run, with my hands tied behind me, but I put on more speed than I'd have thought possible.

I paid no mind to the viney nettles that stung my ankles. I hardly felt the goat-head burs stabbing the soles of my bare feet. I didn't bother about getting mistaken for an Indian and shot at again. All I had on my mind was seeing the kill.

I didn't expect to catch up and get in on it; but maybe if I ran fast enough, I'd get to *see* it.

I ran fast enough, and I saw it. I topped out a little high knoll; and there, strung out before me not more than half a mile off, was the battle, with Indians screeching, soldiers yelling, guns booming, and arrows flying. It was a running fight and a real slaughter.

But it was all going the wrong way. What was getting slaughtered was horses and soldiers!

It was a repeat, on a bigger scale, of what had taken place when the Indians had jumped the two horse raisers. The soldiers killed the horses, while the Indians killed the soldiers.

All my life I'd been told that Indians couldn't shoot for shucks, but here I learned better. I saw the soldiers spill from their saddles, one after another. Time and again, I saw an Indian's horse shot from under him; but always the Indian hit running, and only seconds later was mounted again and hanging down the off side of the horse, where the soldier's bullets couldn't reach him.

The sight was so sickening that I quit watching it. I didn't have to see the soldiers falling or a gap widening between them and the fleeing Indians to know how the fight would wind up.

I looked ahead, searching through the white puffs of gunsmoke. I caught a glimpse of Lisbeth's blond hair glinting in the sun. For just a moment, the curved black horns of Little Arliss's buffalo headdress stood out sharp against the skyline. Then both swept out of sight, swallowed up by distance and the tall waving grass.

I hadn't cried when the Indians captured us. I hadn't cried when they tormented me or when they slaughtered old Jumper. Up to this time, I'd fought back when I could and endured when I couldn't.

But to see Lisbeth and Little Arliss disappear into that vast, wild, unknown land, to realize how little and defenseless they were against the cruel savages they rode with—that was too much. I dropped to the ground and cried like a baby—while over and around me, the grass went right on nodding and whispering, like the tearing hurt inside me had no meaning at all.

Just when I left the knoll and wandered back down to water, I don't know. I was in too much of a daze. All I remember is going back to one of the potholes and drinking, then crawling out into waist-deep water, where I lay with my head on a grass bank, watching some black, yellow-legged mud daubers digging up little balls of mud at the water's edge, listening to the swelling scream of cicadas singing in the mesquites, knowing the kind of despair that goes beyond all resentment and rage.

I'd lost Lisbeth and Little Arliss. I'd been all the protection they'd had against what lay in store for them, yet I'd failed. Now Lisbeth—quiet, shy little Lisbeth—would become the squaw of that stinking Broken Nose, if she was that lucky. And Arliss? Give them time, and they'd not only make him Indian, they'd have him *thinking* Indian. Long before he was grown, he'd be raiding and killing and lifting scalps with the best of their warriors.

I was done. I was whipped. I could think on such things and not even feel the urge to cry any more. One way or another, I could manage to get back home, but I felt no desire to do so. With Lisbeth and Little Arliss lost, I didn't care if I never saw home again—or even if I lived.

*Sam*

# Eight

I WAS so far gone, I might have let Sam get past without ever knowing he was there except for a piece of pure luck. After passing up a dozen good drinking places, Sam left the trail long enough to come and lap water out of the very pothole I lay in.

It wasn't till I *saw* him that I realized how long I'd been hearing his coming.

I lunged to my feet. "Sam!" I yelled at the top of my voice. *"Sam!"*

It startled Sam. I guess it was surprise enough to have startled anything, the way I jumped up and yelled, then started running toward him, knocking water in every direction.

Sam backed off. His hackles rose. He bared his teeth and growled a warning for me to keep my distance.

I stopped, as startled now as Sam had been. I couldn't believe it, him backing off and growling, like I was some sort of dangerous varmint.

"Sam!" I shouted at him. "What's the matter with you?"

I started toward him again. Sam backed a step further, then crouched low to the ground. His eyes took on a glassy

73

shine and there was an even bigger threat in his growl this time.

I stopped, ready to cry.

*"Sam!"* I wailed. "Don't you know me? I'm Travis!"

But Sam didn't know me and wasn't about to let me come any closer. I stood where I was, staring at him, till finally I understood what the trouble was.

A dog's faith in his eyesight is mighty frail. His belief in what he hears isn't a whole lot stronger. What he mainly depends on is his nose; and what he can't scent, he's not going to put much trust in. Especially, out in wild country like this, with danger on every hand.

How could I expect Sam to recognize me? Me, lunging up out of the water, naked as a skinned rabbit, running toward him, hollering my head off—and the wind in the wrong direction for him to catch my scent. It's a wonder he hadn't already jumped me!

I turned and went wading downstream, half circling Sam, talking to him as I went, so full of new hope that it seemed like I'd pop wide open.

"All right, Sam," I told him. "Stay where you are. Hold what you got. Keep trying to bluff me off. Just wait till I get downwind from you. Then I'm coming out of here; and if you're butt-headed enough to jump me, I'll pick me up a club and knock some sense into your fool head."

That was sure a big threat to carry out, with my hands still tied, but it was just blowhard talk. It didn't mean a thing, except that I was so happy to see that old flop-eared, big-jointed dog that I didn't have good sense.

Sam watched me with a wary eye as I waded downstream; but I could tell before I over got to where I wanted that he was beginning to suspect who I was. His hackles flattened along his backbone. His curled-back lips sagged, hiding his bared fangs. Gradually, he rose from his crouch and stood there, beginning to prick up his ears with interest.

I waded to where the wind ripples ran across the water straight from me to Sam. I stood there long enough for him to get a full load of my scent and give it consideration. Then I called to him.

"All right, Sam," I said. "Here I come!"

He knew me then. He let out a little whimpering whine.

He wrung his stub tail so hard he twisted his whole rump end. He cut loose with a loud bawl; and here he came, plunging in high leaps through water too deep for good wading and too shallow for swimming. Wild with joy, he leaped at me, slamming into my chest with the force of a runaway horse. He knocked the wind out of me and tumbled me flat on my back. Then he was all over me, whimpering and yelling and pawing, shoving me under, then slapping me in the face with his big old slobbery tongue every time I got my head up. He was so happy about our meeting, it looked for a minute like he was going to drown me.

Then I got my head up and my wind back and shouted at him, "Sam, you big old ox! Get off of me!"

Sam got off, giving me a chance to get up and wade toward the bank. Only, he still couldn't keep from playnipping at my heels and reaching out to hook a forefoot around one of my ankles, all but tripping me every step I took.

"Cut it out, Sam!" I ordered and kicked him away.

So he let me alone till I reached the bank. Then he played the same old trick he always played on me and Arliss after we'd been swimming and got out and put our clothes on. He sneaked up real close and shook himself, popping his ears, and showering me all over with a fine spray of water.

But this time the joke was on him. He couldn't dirty my clothes. I didn't have any on!

He backed off, getting set to look pitiful and put-upon. He knew he had a scolding coming. When it didn't come, he seemed puzzled and about half disappointed.

I called him over and told him to stand still. I examined the wound in his back. The tomahawk had made a bad gash that looked deep enough to have crippled him, but hadn't. The wound was well clotted over and I couldn't see any blowfly sign.

Before I'd quite finished, Sam did a thing that most dogs can't do. He turned around and looked me square in the eye, and his gaze didn't waver. There was a question in his eyes, the same question that was already beginning to drive me crazy. It was: *When do we get going?*

Well, I was ready to go now. But how was I to go anywhere or do anything with my hands tied behind me?

Sam didn't give me much time to figure out that problem. After handing me that one straight, questioning look, he got restless. He whined. He circled me a couple of times. Then he struck out through the sunflowers and scrub mesquite. A minute later, I heard him open with that high-singing trail cry.

I jumped to my feet in sudden panic.

"Wait, Sam!" I called after him. "Come back here, Sam!"

All the answer I got was that high-singing voice as he opened a second time.

Then I knew Sam wasn't coming back and he wasn't waiting. Not for me or anybody else. He'd gone back and picked up the trail of Little Arliss, and he aimed to hang with that trail as long as there was a trace of scent to follow.

The thought of being left behind, of being alone again, filled me with terror. I went running after Sam, straining frantically at the rawhide binding that held my hands together.

The way my hands came loose might have seemed like a miracle if I hadn't felt so silly about it. Anybody in his right mind would have known how much rawhide would stretch after all the soaking I'd given it back there in the water.

I freed my hands. I stopped and untied the long strip of rawhide I'd been dragging from my left foot. Then I went racing after Sam, calling encouragement to him.

"Go get 'em, Sam," I urged. "Hang with that trail, boy!"

With hands and feet free, I felt light as a feather. I felt strong enough to keep up with Sam, no matter how fast and far he traveled. I felt like I could run from now on.

I ran, so elated that when I came upon the first dead soldier, lying sprawled in the grass, I passed him by with hardly a glance. Just as I came in sight of the second one, however, I stubbed my toe against a hidden rock, and the pain of it knocked some sense back into my head.

I didn't like what I had to do, but I knew I had to do it. It didn't bother me much, pulling off the trooper's boots

76

nd pants. What gave me the creeps was getting his shirt. t was pinned to him, front and back, with a three-foot rrow sticking clear through. But with Sam's trail cry draw-g further and further away, I had no time to be squeam-sh. I grabbed the bloodied arrowhead and broke it off. I olled the soldier over on his back. I caught hold of the :athered shaft and yanked it clear and flung it aside. Then unbuttoned the shirt, stripped it off, and put it on.

The shirt was too long, the hat too small, the pants too ig in the waist and too short in the legs. But the boots were early a perfect fit, which was the main thing. That, and he six-shooter that hung at my belt and the rifle I carried 1 my hand.

The six-shooter was a Colt .45, the rifle a single-shot reachloading .45-70 Springfield. There was plenty of am-1unition for both.

I wondered if what troopers were left alive would return or their dead or if the Indians might backtrack to lift some calps, but nobody came and I never knew why.

I'd worked fast as I could, but the sun was already down nd Sam's trail cry was coming in mighty faint when I truck out after him again. I couldn't run so fast now. I was acking too big a load. But I didn't mind. I had clothes to rotect me, weapons to fight with, and Sam to lead me to vherever the Indians were taking Lisbeth and Little Arliss.

I kept an eye out for a loose horse as I ran. With a horse inder me—a good stout, grain-fed cavalry horse, or even ne of the weaker horses the Indians had let fall behind— 'd be a lot better off than afoot.

I didn't see any horses, though, except dead ones and a ew lost and whinnying colts. One of the colts was sucking dead mare, and it made me sad, knowing that was the last ime he'd ever get a bait of milk from his mama.

The blue-green of the grass changed to purple as night :ame on, then gradually became silver under the light of the ising moon. I ran through the shining grass, following vherever the rise and fall of Sam's trail voice led me. I set a tiff pace. Sam wasn't a fast trailer, just steady, and I looked o overhaul him before long.

But I didn't.

I could gain on him at times. Every now and then, the pitch and rhythm of his voice would change, telling me that the scent he followed had got mixed up or wiped out. Then he'd be quiet for a while; and I'd throw on a new batch of speed, certain I'd catch him while he circled to pick up the lost trail.

But always, before I got there, he'd open, and off he'd go again, driving sure and steady.

This went on for hours. The sweat poured; it wet my clothes and stung my wounds. The stiff trooper boots wore blisters on my heels. The rifle, the six-shooter, and the canvas belts of ammunition got heavier and heavier. Once, I stumbled and fell flat on my face in the grass. Another time, while crossing a rocky little ravine, I sensed danger in time to leap high and far out off a low ledge. The big rattler's strike missed me by a bare inch and I felt his heavy body slide down off my leg as he drew back, buzzing angrily, coiling for another strike.

I didn't stop to kill him; I couldn't afford the time. I had to catch Sam.

I used that thought like a whiplash to keep me going. I'd keep saying to myself; *I got to catch Sam. I got to catch Sam.*

When the sting went out of that thought, I'd prod myself with another. I'd think: *If that streak-faced Comanche can run all day, I can run all night!* Or, *if I lose Sam, I've lost Lisbeth and Little Arliss!*

I ran till my lungs were on fire and ready to burst. I ran till my legs lost all feeling and became dead stumps jolting the rest of my pain-racked body. I ran till I forgot to goad myself, till I even forgot why I was running. From then on, all that kept me on my feet and still going was that wild, sweet-ringing call of Sam's trail cry.

It was like I was tied to that call, and the pull of it never let up, so that I was led on and on, long after the last of my strength had run out.

I finally caught Sam—but only because he stopped again for water. And if water had been plentiful, I wouldn't have caught him then. I was too far behind.

I got my first sight of him as he stood out in the middle of a broad flat wash that wound through the grass. The bed f the wash was filled with deep sand. In the moonlight, ne sand looked smooth, clean-swept and golden, except for wide, dark streak where the trampling hoofs of hard-riven horses had pitted and rumpled it.

There was no surface water in the sand; all of the flow as underneath. But in one place, the water was so near ne top that it seeped into one of the deeper horse tracks. It as out of this track that Sam was trying to drink.

Some dogs would have known to dig deeper; but Sam ad never before needed to dig for water. What I found him oing, when I came staggering toward him, was lapping up hat little water he could get, then backing off and waiting or the track to fill again.

He whined and wagged his stump tail as I dropped down eside him, gasping for breath. He was glad enough to see ne, but what pleased him even more, it looked like, was for ne to use my hands to claw out a foot-deep hole in the and.

The underground water seeped in faster. Sam shoved in o get the first drink. While he was at it, I slipped the leather elt out of my sagging soldier pants and looped it around is neck. The other end I snapped into the buckle of my ix-shooter belt.

"Now, you rascal," I panted. "You're not getting away rom me again."

I crowded in beside him. We both drank from the same vater hole. Then I rolled over and lay flat on my back in he sand, and couldn't have found more comfort in a bed vith a goose-feather mattress.

From far out in the wilderness of shining grass lifted the nowl of a great gray loafer wolf. Instantly, Sam rose with . snarl.

I reached out and pulled him toward me. "Hush up and ay down," I told him.

He hushed up, but he didn't lie down. Instead, he started nosing over my body, searching out my wounds. I lay with ny sweat-soaked shirt unbuttoned and open, and he could et at some of the worst ones. He started a gentle licking of he wounds, and I didn't stop him. His wet tongue felt soft nd soothing, and I knew from past experience how healing he lick of a dog's tongue can be.

79

The wolf howled again. Sam paid him no mind. And me —well, I fell asleep so fast that I never even heard the last of the howl.

A clawing pain brought me awake. My eyes popped open. I found Sam standing over me, whimpering and whining, pawing my sore body with a forefoot.

I shoved him aside. I sat up and looked around. The sun stood better than an hour high. The morning breeze had already started up and set the grass to whispering.

I was thirsty again. I rolled over and drank from the hole in the sand. Then I tried to get to my feet and almost didn't make it, I was that stiff all over. Also, my soldier clothes were stuck tight to several festering sores that Sam hadn't been able to reach. It all but took my breath to pull my clothes loose.

But these were outside pains, and I'd had them long enough to be used to them. *Inside,* I felt fine. Inside, I felt ready to take up the trail that Sam was so anxious to follow again.

But first, I needed to put Sam on a leash. I'd learned a lesson. Maybe I could run as fast as Sam could trail, but I sure couldn't run for as long at a time. Last night, I'd caught him out of sheer luck. Let him get that big a lead on me again, and my luck might not hold.

Sam kept whining and tugging at my belt, restless to get gone.

"Be still," I scolded.

He hushed and stood waiting while I thought. The belt wouldn't do; it was too short. Anyhow, without it to hold up my oversized pants, they'd be down around my ankles before I'd taken a dozen steps. I considered the cartridge belts, but they were too short.

I looked around, thinking hard. My eye lit on a clump of bear grass growing at the edge of the sandy wash. That's what I needed! Those long green spiny blades were nearly as stout as rawhide. Back home, we always used them for binding bundles of corn-top fodder. Tie a bunch of them together, and they'd make as fine a leash as a body could want.

I headed for the bear grass. Out of pure habit, I reached

into my pocket for a knife to cut the blades—and found one! It would sure make the job easier. I went to cutting the blades and knotting them together. Each blade was better than a foot long. Twelve to fifteen would be a-plenty.

I was done with making the leash when I heard a rustling in the grass. I stiffened. I reached for my rifle lying beside me, then noticed Sam. He'd heard the sound, too. He stood with his muzzle lifted, his ears pricked up. But he didn't raise a hackle, and he didn't growl. I knew then that whatever made the rustling sound was no threat to us. Just some varmint, I guessed.

I tied the leash around Sam's neck. I worked the belt through the loops in my pants, drew up the slack, and buckled it. Then I led Sam through the grass to see what was making those odd clicking and clacking sounds—like pieces of dry wood being slapped together.

I made a cautious approach, holding my rifle ready.

What I found was a couple of dry-land terrapins. They were big ones, with shells the size of dinner plates. And they were fighting—I guess. I'd never seen terrapins fight; and if this was a fight, it was the most peculiar one I ever watched.

Best I could tell, all either terrapin had in mind was to flop the other one over on his back. It was a real curiosity to watch them. I wondered how a terrapin could know that once he was turned upside down, he'd be helpless.

Suddenly, my interest in the terrapins took a different turn. I remembered a long-winded yarn old man Searcy had once told about eating roasted terrapins with some friendly Kiowas. I hadn't eaten since I'd choked down a few bites of old Jumper the day before I was hungry.

With a rifle, I could kill game; but let me start shooting around, and the Indians were sure to hear the shots and send somebody back to get me.

It seemed shameful to kill something as helpless as these old terrapins. But I crushed their shells with my rifle butt. I gutted them with my pocketknife. I sliced the good meat away from the broken shells and divided it with Sam.

We ate it raw. We didn't have time for cooking, even if I could have built a fire with sticks, like the Indians, which I doubted.

The meat smelled pretty rank and was tough to chew; but I ate it, and my stomach held it, and I felt confident that it would give me strength to keep going.

Getting Sam back on the trail was no problem. The horse tracks were plain in the sandy wash; and it didn't take him but a minute to nose out the scent he wanted.

He wrung his stub tail. He threw up his head and opened with his bell-ringing voice. Then he took a sudden spurt ahead, and that's when the trouble started.

Sam had never before run a trail while on a leash; and when he hit the end of that string and got jerked up short, he threw a wall-eyed fit.

He was worse than Little Arliss when he got mad. He wheeled around, snapping and snarling at the string. He reared up and threw his weight against it, trying to break loose. He hit the ground, wallowing and screeching. He leaped high into the air and turned a somersault. He ran circles around me, yelping and pitching and bawling. The capers he cut, you'd have thought he was a bull calf that had been roped for the first time.

I kept hanging to the leash and shouting at him, telling him to cut out that foolishness and behave himself. For all the good it did, I could have been hollering straight into a big wind.

I don't know how I'd ever have got him stopped if he hadn't taken a second wallowing fit and wrapped himself up in that string so tight he couldn't move.

Then when I got my hands on him, I didn't know what to do. If I turned him loose, he'd get away from me. If he kept fighting that leash, we sure couldn't get anywhere. And to keep messing with him like this, I ran the risk of getting him so aggravated he'd quit the trail for good.

I sat and studied on it a good long while.

So far, all I'd done was fuss at him. What if I took time off and explained the situation, telling him what had to be done and why?

It seemed worth a try. Sam was a butt head and always would be. If he hadn't been, he'd never have hung with the trail this far. On the other hand, he'd never been a dang fool, either.

I led him back to water. We both drank again out of the same hole. I spoke soft to him and hugged him up and scratched his ears and stroked his back and bragged on him. And, being as greedy for praise as anybody else, Sam lapped it all up like it was a bowl of sweet cream. In no time, I had him so proud of himself, he was wriggling all over and slapping me in the face with a wet tongue to show that we were in complete agreement on what a fine dog he was.

That's when I pushed him away and laid it on the line.

"Now, look, Sam," I said. "We're both after the same thing. We stick together, maybe we can do it. We get split up, we don't have a chance. Them Indians, they'll shoot you and lose me, and that'll be the last anybody'll ever see of Lisbeth and Little Arliss. You understand?"

I don't guess a dog understands many words, but I think he can listen and tell more than a lot of people believe about the feeling back of the words. And right then, I was so desperate to make Sam understand that I'll always believe some of my feelings got through to him.

Anyhow, he stood quiet and heard me out, then whined and came to lay his head on my knee and look up at me, like he was *trying* to understand. So I got up and led him back to the trail and hissed him out, and he took it.

This time I was all set for him. When he opened and spurted forward, I was quick to go with him, giving him plenty of slack line, so he wouldn't get jerked up short again.

And it worked. He opened a second time; and we took off across that great rolling sea of grass, running together, with Sam's bell-clear voice rising and falling with a regularity and sureness that put strength in my muscles and lifted my hopes clear out of all reason.

The sun was high and hot and I was beginning to tire when we came upon a little cluster of cone-shaped hills. Prickly pear grew on their slopes and the green pads of the pear were studded with ripe red apples. At the base of one hill stood a lone mott of scrub live oaks, and the trail we followed led straight toward it.

I was thinking that under those oaks would be a good place for us to shade up till I caught my breath, when Sam's trail cry broke in the middle. He came to a sudden halt, stood stiff-legged, with his hackles rising. He growled.

*Indians,* I thought, and dropped out of sight into the grass.

"Down, Sam!" I said in a low voice. "Get down and keep quiet!"

Sam crouched beside me, still growling.

I felt my body tighten with scare, but there was no panic. If a couple of Apaches had heard Sam and dropped back to make a kill, I'd come for the same thing. Only, I aimed to kill first.

I tried to think what best to do. As things stood now, I couldn't see them, but they had to have spotted the place where I'd dropped into the grass. Pulling Sam along, I started crawling off to one side. I crawled fast, depending on the wind-tossed grass to hide my motion and muffle any sound.

Fifty yards away, I changed course and began a slower, more careful crawl toward the oaks. I planned to carry the fight to the savages from this direction while they watched for me in another.

I was closer to the oaks than I really wanted to be before an opening in the grass allowed me to peer through. But I couldn't see anything; the shade under the trees was too dense.

Then I stiffened. A shadowy form had shifted. Another one moved, and I heard a low grunt. Beside me, Sam uttered another low rumbling growl.

"Sh-h-h-h!" I shushed him and he hushed, but it was plain he didn't like the setup.

I eased my rifle to my shoulder and waited. I wanted that first shot to count. After that, if they rushed me, I'd have to depend on the six-shooter and I wasn't too sure of myself with it.

A figure moved again, taking shape against a patch of sunlight on the far side of the mott. Best I could tell, one of the savages had lifted his head for a look around. I thought I saw a feather sticking up out of his hair.

I drew a fine bead on that head and squeezed off. The gun barked. The butt slammed against my shoulder. Black-powder gunsmoke fogged the air and through the fog came what sounded like the squeal of a stuck pig. Then the thicket exploded, and here they came—not Indians at all, but a band of javelina hogs!

I lunged up, bug-eyed with surprise, as they rushed me, coughing and roaring, popping gleaming white teeth. Then the mass of them cut my feet from under me, trampling me with their little hard hoofs, slashing at me with razor-sharp tusks. Their rank musky scent all but choked off my breath before I could scramble back to my feet and start clubbing them off with my rifle butt.

It was Sam who saved me, partly by dealing out more punishment, mostly by making more noise. His loud roars and savage snarls as he battled the hogs seemed to attract the fierce little animals away from me to him.

The pack around me thinned. I saw a chance to run and took it. I tore out around the slope of that hill, yelling as I ran, "Run, Sam! Run!"

When I looked back, I saw that Sam had thrown the fight to the javelinas and was high-tailing it through the grass, with the pigs chasing after him. Sam was leading away from me. Maybe he knew he could outrun those nasty little fighters and I couldn't.

I quit running and sat down on a little rock ledge to catch my breath. I felt a stinging pain across my left foot and glanced down to find a long slash in the leather across the instep of my boot. I pulled the boot off and examined my foot. There was a bleeding groove in the flesh, but the cut wasn't deep. I examined myself for more wounds, but all I found was my six-shooter belt cut nearly in two.

I'd come out lucky. Javelinas on the prod can be nearly as dangerous as razorback range hogs.

While I waited for Sam to come back, I thought what a fool stunt I'd pulled. Letting my imagination get the upper hand of me so that I'd mistaken javelinas for Indians. Alone in a wild country like this, a body couldn't afford such mistakes. Any one could be his last.

I told myself that, from now on, I'd watch closer and think quicker. I'd be sharp-eyed and wary, dangerous as any wild animal. I wouldn't let myself get caught short a second time.

And while I sat there, telling myself these things, I was making the worst mistake yet.

It wasn't till the faint sound of Sam's trail cry came floating back to me from far out on the prairie that I realized what I'd done.

I started up in panic. "Sam!" I called. "Sam!"

I went plunging down the slope, sick with knowing what a fool I'd been. I set a pace that I couldn't possibly hold, yet I knew I had to hold it if I hoped to keep in hearing distance of Sam.

For Sam was back on the trail of Little Arliss and had no time to lose.

I lasted for maybe an hour before the ground began to rock and heave under me, making me stumble. I slowed then, hoping for the dizzy spell to pass. Instead, the ground rose up and slammed me in the face, and I went spinning far out into some great dark and empty place where not even the call of Sam's trail cry could reach me any more.

*Papa*

*Nine*

A HAND touched my face. I started up in terror. Crouched over me, black against the blinding sunlight, was a man figure.

Like a trapped animal, I lunged up and clutched his throat, choking off his shout of alarm.

He threw himself backward, dragging me with him. He clawed desperately at my hands, and other hands joined his, all seeking to break the strangle hold I held.

But I was too strong. All of me—all the rage and pain and fear and loneliness and awful despair I'd known—was in my hands, and no force on earth had the strength to break their grip.

Then, through the shouts and confusion and my blind rage to kill, Papa's voice reached me.

"Travis!" he was shouting. "Turn him loose, boy. Turn him loose, I say!"

That broke the spell. It took away my strength. Big Burn Sanderson was now able to break my grasp on Herb Haley's throat, and I looked on in stunned surprise as Haley flung himself aside and lay in the grass, sucking for air in great raspy gasps.

Sanderson was squatted on his heels beside me. He still held my hands, but his blue eyes were as warm and friendly as ever. He glanced over my head and said in a joking voice, "Be dog, Jim, I hope this boy don't never take a sudden dislike to me!"

Then I knew whose strong arms held me from behind.

"Papa!" I cried.

I whirled, jerking free of Sanderson, getting a glimpse of several Salt Licks settlers before looking up into Papa's familiar face. Then the tears came, blurring everything, and the shivers got me, so that I just lay back in Papa's arms, crying and shaking all over.

Papa held me close. "It's all right, boy," he comforted. "Just take it easy for a minute and you'll be all right."

"Give him some water," somebody said, and I recognized Ben Todd's voice.

I heard the slosh of water inside the canteen and the squeal of a metal cap being unscrewed. I dragged my shirt sleeve across my eyes, wiping away the tears, and reached a shaky hand for the canteen. I lifted it and let the water, with its stale, tinny taste, go rattling down my parched throat.

Old man Searcy hawked and spat, like he always did before spinning some long-winded yarn.

"Puts me in mind of a time I'm on a cow hunt in the cedar brakes west of Hornsby's Bend," he began. "Dry as a powderhouse, the country is, and—"

"Not now, Mr. Searcy," Papa interrupted.

Searcy said in a complaining voice, "Well, all I aimed to tell was how them dogs of our'n—"

"It'll keep, Mr. Searcy," Sanderson cut in.

Mention of dogs made me jerk the canteen from my mouth. I came to my feet.

"Sam!" I cried out. "We got to catch Sam!"

Sanderson came to his feet with me. He asked, "How big a lead you think he's got?"

I glanced up at the sun. "It's hard to tell," I said. "An hour—maybe two. Don't know for certain when I blacked out."

Lester White moved in to peer at me with a questioning look in his black eyes. White was a newcomer to Salt Licks.

He was from Virginia, in search of grassland on which to raise fine horses. He was young and handsome and rode better horses and wore finer clothes than anybody else. He talked different from us, too. Some settlers looked on him as being a dandy, with too much book learning to have any sense.

Now he said, "Apparently, young man, you are saying that a dog has been on this trail for more than forty-eight hours."

"Yes, sir," I said. "Sam's been trailing Little Arliss from the start."

White backed off, looking thoughtful. "That's hard to believe," he said.

Papa looked to Sanderson. "You think we can catch him before night?" he asked.

"If we hump it," Sanderson said. "But we'll be whipping over and under if that old pot-hound pup's got more than a two-hour lead."

A sudden thought hit Papa. He felt of my forehead. He pulled aside one half of my unbuttoned shirt. He stared at my skin, now fiery with sunburn. He saw the swollen, festering sores made by the Indians' firebrands. He got gray in the face.

"This boy's not able to ride," he said to Sanderson. "Feel of him. Look at this!"

" 'Course I can ride!" I protested.

His eyes grave with concern, Sanderson pulled open the other side of my shirt. The men all crowded in close, staring at my wounds in fearful awe.

Lester White's black eyes flashed me a quick look of sympathy. Uncle Pack Underwood, a lean old wolf of a man, turned away to stare out across the prairie, his lined face bleak with a dark and brooding bitterness. Bud Searcy went all to pieces. Tears spilled down his bearded cheeks and his lips started quivering.

"My grandbaby!" he cried out. "My pore little grandgirl! Have they abused her?"

"Not yet," I said. "I got a knife into the one that tried it. He won't try again—for a while! But Little Arliss—they got him stripped naked. And he keeps fighting back!"

Sanderson dropped my shirt and shook his head. "He's bad hurt, all right," he said to Papa.

" 'Course I'm hurt!" I flared. "I been hurt since night before last. But it hasn't stopped me, has it?"

"The boy's got guts," Ben Todd said. Todd was a shy, heavy-set man who said little and spent most of his time wild-bee hunting.

"No question," Lester White agreed.

Any other time, I'd have felt proud of such a compliment, but right now it didn't matter what anybody thought.

"I tell you, we've got to catch Sam!" I said. "He's hot on the trail of Little Arliss!"

Sanderson nodded and turned to Papa. "He's right," he said. "We sure need to overhaul that dog."

Herb Haley got to his feet, rubbing his throat and still eyeing me warily. I felt bad about trying to choke him, but it seemed like he ought to make allowance for the shape I was in.

Uncle Pack said, "We could grease the boy. That'd help some."

Papa looked doubtful—and desperate. He said to me, "You think you could make it, son? If we greased you good, all over?"

"He's *got* to make it!" Searcy said wildly. "I tell you, if them heathen abuse my little grandgirl—"

He broke down without finishing and went to crying.

I said to Papa, "Forget the greasing. We got no time."

"We'll take time," Sanderson said. He turned to Herb Haley. "Herb, will you slice the rind off that side of bacon in my saddlebag?"

Herb Haley was still keeping an eye on me, like he expected me to jump him again.

"Allow me!" Lester White said. He went for the bacon rind.

Papa and Sanderson started stripping me.

Wiley Crup, a squint-eyed man with a squirrel mouth and the figure of a sand-hill crane, came to stand over us. Across his shoulder, muzzle forward, he packed a rifle about the size and weight of a crowbar. It was a .50 caliber Sharps, used for buffalo hunting.

Now, he set the butt of his rifle to the ground and laid

a forearm across the muzzle. He leaned his weight on the gun while he stared at Sanderson.

"Was I ramroding this hunt," he said, "which I ain't—not even being considered for election—I might point out a little matter what's being overlooked."

Sanderson glanced at him. "Speak your piece, Wiley," he invited. "We ain't above listening."

"Well, here's the thing," Wiley drawled. "We start out on this siwash hunt with eight men on eight horses. We pick up this boy—who aims to ride double?"

All were silent a moment, considering, before Ben Todd said, "Couldn't we swap about?"

"Not the way Sanderson threatens to travel," Crup declared. "We ride at that pace, a double load'll have ever' horse in this outfit dragging out his tracks by sundown."

I never had liked Wiley Crup. He was always too contentious and suspicious of everything and everybody. And after he'd taken up hide hunting a couple of years back, you'd have thought he was the only man ever to shoot a buffalo or see an Indian.

I said, hot with resentment, "I'll take it afoot. I'll run, holding to somebody's stirrup. Like the Comanche."

"Comanch!" Crup exclaimed. He whirled on Sanderson. "You said they was Pache!" he charged. "Said you could tell by the sign!"

Sanderson shot me a puzzled look.

"They *are* Apaches," I said. "All but one. He's Comanche. Somebody shot him, back there where they caught us. It hurt him to ride, so he—"

Sanderson cut in. "Thought that one looked Comanche, when I fired on him."

Crup snorted his disbelief. "How come a Comanch raidin' with a bunch of Paches? Everybody knows they're mortal enemies."

Sanderson shrugged. *"Quién sabe?"* he said. "A loner, most likely. Hubbed trouble with his own tribe, maybe, and threw in with the Apaches."

"Yeah, maybe!" Crup sneered. "And maybe you don't know sic 'em about the sign you read."

Sanderson paid no more mind to Crup's insult than he

would do to a worrisome gnat, but Uncle Pack spoke up in a raspy voice.

"Wiley," he said, "you ain't to blame for being born a fool. That weren't yore doing. But it wouldn't hurt you none if you tried to overcome the handicap."

Crup's face darkened with resentment.

"The main question is," Sanderson said, "can we overhaul that dog before dark. With Sam, we can trail all night. Without him, we'll have to wait around for daylight."

Papa started rubbing the bacon rind gently over my body. The curing salt stung my wounds, but I knew that it and the grease would help to heal them.

"As for Travis," Sanderson went on, "he's young, and tough as an old boot heel. Feed and water him, and he'll make it. Won't you, boy?"

He grinned and winked at me.

It was just a little thing; yet sometimes, just a little is all a body needs to pull himself back together. Burn Sanderson was my friend. He had confidence in me. That alone was enough to lift my spirits and help me to throw off the shakes.

Also, there was a big belly-filling bait of grub they fed me. Fried salt-cured bacon. Corn-meal hoecakes cooked in the grease after the bacon was done. It was cold leftovers from the last meal they'd eaten. It was salty. It was greasy. It had a little sand and some ashes in it. It was hardscrabble, pore folks' grub that, back home, nobody ate except at the tail end of winter when game was scarce and the range cattle were thin.

Yet I gobbled it down like it was a Christmas dinner with all the fixings. It was exactly what I needed, especially the salt. You keep pouring out sweat like I'd done for the last couple of days and nights, and pretty soon your body gets to craving salt almost worse than a good meal.

While I ate, the men hammered at me with questions. I answered between bites. When I came to the part about the Indian and soldier fight, Sanderson shook his head.

"Injuns all armed with modern rifles, I guess?"

"Yes, sir," I said. "Mostly Henry .44's."

"That's the army for you," he said. "Sending troops out

92

with single-shot Springfields to face sixteen-shot repeaters. Poor devils didn't have a chance."

Wiley Crup snorted with contempt. "Far as I'm con-sarned," he said, patting the scarred stock of his monster rifle, "all them fancy, new-fangled guns can be throwed in the creek. Me, I'm sticking to this old Christian Sharps britch-loading Big Fifty."

"But gosh dog, Wiley," Herb Haley exclaimed. "Pack-ing that much artillery, it's enough to make your horse swaybacked."

"Maybe," Crup said smugly. "But she can accommodate a paper cartridge, a linen one, or just plain loose powder and lead. It's all the same to her. She'll still pack a ball a thousand yards. I've kilt buffler at better'n five hundred."

Papa wanted to know more about the Comanche. Finally, he said to Sanderson: "Burn, if that Indian can run like that, we can. And it'd sure sàve on horseflesh."

"I'm ready to take my turn," Lester White said. "I'm as fit as any man alive."

Sanderson sized up White's trim figure. "You look it, Mr. White," he said. "But dealing with Injuns, a man can turn up some real surprises."

"We can sure give it a try," Papa persisted.

Sanderson nodded and got to his feet. "And if we hope to catch that dog before dark," he said, "it's time we got on the move."

Every man in the outfit was well mounted, even to Bud Searcy, who'd borrowed a big old apron-faced sorrel from Papa, a horse that wasn't much to look at, but one with plenty of staying power. Compared, however, to the proud-stepping, catfooted bay that Lester White rode, all our horses looked scrubby as Indian ponies. White called the bay a "hunter," whatever that meant, and one glance at the long clean lines of him told you that here was a horse to take you there and bring you back, and do it in a hurry.

Sanderson mounted me on his horse and hung his spurs and gun gear to the saddle horn. Papa tried to argue with him, claiming Sanderson ought to stay mounted all the time, him being the only real tracker in the outfit.

But Sanderson wouldn't listen. "I'm young and fast afoot," he said. "And a one-eyed candy peddler could trail that many horses running through green grass. Anyhow, I been elected boss of this outfit, and I ain't yet had a chance to throw my weight around."

He grinned up at Papa, spanked the rump of his horse, and said, "Let's go!"

So we took off, riding hard, with Papa in the lead, with Sanderson holding to my stirrup, with me gritting my teeth against the pain of the saddle.

In spite of the pain, I felt a lot better. I wasn't alone any more; and I no longer had to carry the full load of responsibility for Lisbeth and Little Arliss.

Sanderson ran for better than an hour before he gave under the strain. He didn't say anything, but I began to feel the pull of him on my stirrup. I called ahead to Papa, and Sanderson didn't argue when Papa reined up and Lester White insisted on taking Sanderson's place.

Sanderson wiped the streaming sweat from his face with his shirt sleeve and shook his head.

"I got to admit," he panted, "I ain't the man that Comanche is."

"I expect none of us are," Papa said. "Not on foot, anyhow."

White said nothing, but looked determined to show himself the equal of any man, red or white. He ran, holding to Sanderson's stirrup, for maybe fifteen minutes longer than Sanderson had. Then he, too, had to give it up.

When he could get back his breath, he asked, "How long at a time did this Comanche run?"

"Half a day," I told him.

He stared at me in astonishment. "At a pace this swift?"

"Not always," I said. "Most of the time, though."

"And packing a rifle ball in one leg," Sanderson pointed out with a wry grin.

That knocked some of the little-rooster strut out of Lester White. But he was man enough to take it without making excuses. He mounted up, looking thoughtful and a bit shaken, and offered a stirrup to Ben Todd.

Todd surprised us all. To look at the chunky bee hunter, nobody would have figured him for a runner. Yet, with short legs flying, he held the stiff pace we'd set for mile after mile without any evidence of strain, so that I began to think he could equal the Comanche.

But after better than a couple of hours, he, too, had to call it quits and let Herb Haley take over.

Following Haley, the others took turns, even to Bud Searcy, who was outraged when Papa and Sanderson tried to tell him he was too old.

"I didn't come along to be a drag on this chase," he declared.

So we kept driving, nine men and eight horses, pushing to the limit of endurance, traveling across a rolling sea of grass so vast that it seemed to have no beginning and no end, moving under a spread of sky that stretched out beyond any distance a body could bring himself to believe. And still the trail led on.

The sun sank lower. Men and horses began to lag. Papa's face, grim and determined up to now, began to take on a bleak, anxious look. I fought a losing fight with the dread mounting inside me.

For, with the coming of sunset, the cross wind that had blown all day shut down, leaving hardly a ripple on the grass. Now, I could no longer tell myself that the wind was carrying Sam's voice away from us. Now, I had to face up to the fact that night would soon set in, blotting out the trail, and we still hadn't come within hearing distance of Sam.

Then Sanderson shouted and pointed. I looked ahead. Far out against the sinking sun, I saw a swirl of buzzards. They were dipping and diving, only to rise again on great flapping wings. They circled low above the grass, evidently wanting to settle down, but kept scared off by a danger we couldn't see.

I snatched at a new hope. That could be Sam out yonder! He could have stopped to feed on the carcass of some animals the Indians had shot for meat. It might be him, keeping the buzzards fought off.

It turned out to be Sam, all right. And there was plenty of meat for him to feed on. Scattered about in the little swag where we found him lay the skinned carcasses of eighteen buffalo.

But Sam wasn't feeding on any of the meat. He was too busy fighting off a snarling pack of gray loafer wolves.

The minute we rode in sight, it was easy to read the setup. The wolves had been feeding on the dead buffalo. Sam, intent on following the trail of Little Arliss, had come charging down upon them before he knew they were there. The wolves had jumped him, and they'd been too many for him. Sam had fought his way to the fallen trunk of a dead willow that lay at the edge of a buffalo wallow. There, backed up against the log, where the gnarled, upthrust roots protected his rump, he'd made his stand.

With rump and one side protected, he fought with his head extended, with his forefeet drawn far back under his body, making his legs hard to get at. He met each charge with a roar and a frenzy of cutting and slashing that sent wolf after wolf reeling back, screeching with pain. Yet, with his other side wide open, so that two or three wolves could rush him at once, it was still just a matter of time before one of them locked jaws with him and dragged him out to where the others could hamstring and cut him to pieces.

It was the uproar of Sam's battle with the wolves that had the buzzards disturbed. Now, the big ugly birds circled higher as we went rushing in, and the black shadows of their wings glided across the grass.

*Travis*

## Ten

I LED the charge toward the fight and drew my six-shooter, aiming to kill me some wolves. Others did the same. But Sanderson called out, telling us to hold our fire.

"Whip 'em off with your catch ropes," he yelled.

We holstered our guns and reached down ropes of braided rawhide. We shook out loops and swung them high. And the snarling pack, bent on killing Sam, paid us no mind until we were among them.

Our loops whistled as they cut through the air. Surprised wolves yelped and fell away from the sting of our lashings. They wallowed and pitched and screeched. Men shouted. Excited horses squealed and lunged and lashed out with their heels.

It was over and done with, almost before it started. The routed pack scattered and slunk to cover.

Wiley Crup complained in a sour voice, "With guns, we could a-kilt 'em."

"And brung down a whole passel of redskins on our necks," Uncle Pack pointed out. "Was any in hearing range."

I looked down at Sam. He was still crouched half under

97

the log, staring at us. He looked worse surprised than the time, back home, when he started to shake an old mama possum to death and slung a whole shower of baby possums loose from her pouch.

His look was so comical that even Papa grinned a little as the two of us dismounted and walked toward him.

"Sam!" Papa called to him in a warm voice. "Come here, you big old ugly devil!"

Such familiar talk broke Sam's trance. Here he came, charging us like a lumbering bull. He bawled a welcome, which likely had as much to do with his relief at being saved from the wolves as it did with his joy in seeing us.

But if Sam's pleasure in the meeting was partly selfish, so was ours. In fact, I felt almost grateful to the wolves. They'd held Sam up long enough for us to overtake him. Now, I figured, our chances for catching up with the Indians were at least double what they'd been.

So me and Papa squatted on our heels and let Sam lick and maul us around and spatter blood all over us—like we were the greatest people on earth.

Finally, I caught and held him so we could look him over. He had a deep gash across the bridge of his nose, and one ear had been cut to ribbons. Both wounds leaked considerable blood, but neither was crippling.

Lester White came up and looked Sam over, making a careful study of him from every angle. At last, he asked, "What are his blood lines, Mr. Coates?"

Sanderson, walking past, answered for Papa. "That Sam," he said, "is a Genuine Amalgamated Pot-Hound." Without cracking a smile, he moved on, leaving White looking doubtful.

"I don't believe I'm familiar with the breed," he said uncertainly.

Papa rose to his feet. For the moment, his face was relaxed, and I saw the old familiar twinkle in his eyes.

"It's not an uncommon one," he said, "here in Texas."

He left and walked out through the grass, as if searching for something.

It was good to see Papa smile again. Even for just that little bit. It was proof that our catching up with Sam had lifted his hopes.

A moment later, he was back, packing an old sun-dried buffalo chip. He broke it into pieces. He crushed and rolled the pieces between his hands till they became trashy dust. He started spilling the dust down over Sam's wounds.

White watched in puzzled silence. When the dust clotted and checked the flow of blood, he exclaimed, "Amazing! Truly amazing."

While all this went on, Sanderson was giving orders for pitching camp.

"We'll eat and rest our horses," he said, "then pull out along about moonrise."

He sent Herb Haley and Ben Todd riding out to scout the higher ground and told the others to slip the bridle bits from the mouths of their horses so they could drink and get some graze.

"And you better tie up that old pup," he called to me and Papa. "We don't want him taking off on that trail again till we're ready to go with him."

All that was left of the bear-grass leash I'd made for Sam was the part tied around his neck. So Papa brought a rope, and we tied Sam to the willow log.

"Now, you stay with him," Papa ordered, "and make sure he don't gnaw that rope in two." He peered at me closer. "You hurting much?"

"Some," I said. "Mostly, I'm just tired and hungry."

Sanderson and old man Searcy came up.

Sanderson said, "Might better strip him and let him lay in that water till we get supper. Water's mighty healing for the sort of wounds he's got."

"That's sure a fact," Searcy declared. "Don't know how many old winter sores I've cured, once spring come and the water warmed up enough I could run a trotline for catfish. I'm fixing to give my old beat-up feet a good soaking right now."

Searcy sat down with a grunt and began pulling off his boots. White looked at the brackish, green-scum water and then back at Sanderson.

"Do you mean to say," he asked, "that water as filthy as this possesses curative powers?"

Sanderson nodded. "Sometimes," he said, "it looks like the nastier it is, the better it heals."

"It ought to cool his fever, anyhow," Papa said.

So they helped me out of my sweaty soldier clothes and spread them out on the log to dry.

Some buffalo had wallowed a pothole in the mud beside the log. Black water had seeped back into the hole, filling it. I waded out and lay down. The water was sun-warmed and stank of rot. The bottom ooze was soft and slimy.

I thought to myself, *If filthy water is healing, this ought to cure me.* But I had to admit that as it closed over my sore body, it sure *felt* healing.

Old man Searcy sat on the log and soaked his feet in the wallow. Papa and Sanderson stomped dead branches from the log. White helped carry the broken pieces to a dried-up edge of the wallow where the grass didn't grow and they built up a campfire. Others brought their possible bags and from them produced a coffee pot, corn meal for making hoecakes, side meat, and a pan to fry in. The horses, with bridles hanging to their saddle horns, waded out into the dirty water to drink, then drifted away to graze.

I lay in the water and looked past a couple of green willows growing at the edge of the wallow, watching the sun go down. As it sank behind a cloud bank, it shot great banners of light high into the sky. The banners flamed red, pink, yellow, and green.

I lay back and fitted my head into a crotch between the roots of the willow log. I caught my first smell of boiling coffee and frying meat and thought to myself that I'd get up in a minute and go eat.

When I woke up, fireflies were cutting the darkness with glowing streaks of light. Little frogs were piping. From the willows came the lonely quavering cries of screech owls. From out on the prairie rose the mournful howls of the wolves, gathering to feed on the dead buffalo once we'd stomped out the fire and gone. And, from beside the fire, came Uncle Pack's voice, harsh with a wild bitterness.

"Don't argue me the right or wrong of Injun killing!" he was shouting. "I see my cabin burning like a bresh pile. I see my woman and two childer kilt and sculped . . . Now, I kill Injuns!"

I'd heard Uncle Pack's story before, but it seemed to hit me harder this time.

After a long silence, Burn Sanderson spoke in a quiet voice.

"I wasn't trying to argue you out of Injun killing, Uncle Pack," he said. "I was just explaining how killing off the buffalo makes the Injun fight back all the worse. He's lived off the buffalo for too long. Since way back before the Spanish brung in the horse, he's lived off the buffalo. Afoot, he hung to the flanks of the big herds like the wolf packs, and went where they went. Horseback, he done the same.

"He et the buffalo's meat. He drunk his blood. He used his hide for clothes and shelter and bedding. He strung bows with his hamstrings, made tomahawks and knives out of his bone. He even boiled the sap out of his horns and hoofs for glue."

"The siwash don't own the buffler," Wiley Crup said. "Don't nobody own the buffler."

"Maybe he don't earmark and brand, like we do cattle," Sanderson said. "But after hundreds of years—maybe thousands—the Injun *feels* that he owns him."

"Well, he can learn to feel different," Crup declared.

I saw Sanderson get to his feet. He said to Papa, "Jim, you better go wake the boy."

I got up then and was washing myself off when Papa came to get me.

"You feel better, son?" he asked.

I nodded.

He helped me into my clothes and we walked toward the fire. I wondered about Burn Sanderson. How come he could kill Indians—and I knew he'd kill them—and still argue that they had a better right to the country and the buffalo than the white man?

Before we reached the fire, Herb Haley asked, "Well, what about them sculped hide hunters me 'n' Ben found out yonder?"

"Leave 'em to the wolves," Sanderson said. "We're out to save a couple of children. Not to bury a bunch of fool buffalo hunters!"

I ate by the faint light of the dying campfire. Again, I ate the salty, greasy food like I couldn't get enough.

"Anybody feed Sam?" I asked.

Sanderson grinned. "Till his eyeballs bulged," he said. "He'll be ready when you are."

I wiped clean the greasy frying pan with a chunk of hoe-cake. I crammed it into my mouth and came to my feet.

"I'm ready now," I said.

Sanderson reached for the frying pan and shoved it into a sack. He turned and called out into the darkness, "Let's go!"

The men came, bringing the horses. Papa went to turn Sam loose and whistle him out. We mounted up, all but Ben Todd, whose turn for running came next.

We sat our saddles and waited while Sam ran swift, widening circles around the camp. In the dark, we couldn't see him; but we could hear him bounding through the grass, hear his loud hasseling as he searched eagerly for the scent he wanted.

Papa said anxiously, "He was crippling pretty bad when I turned him loose."

"Stands to reason," Sanderson said. "All the ground he's covered. But I greased his feet good. And I never yet seen sore feet keep a dog from running a trail."

Out of the darkness rose Sam's voice, stirring a strong feeling inside me.

Sanderson said, "He's got it!"

We moved out, riding fast at first, gradually slowing our pace to fit Sam's. We didn't want to overrun him or crowd him too close from behind.

We came to the wagon of the scalped buffalo hunters. Here the rhythm of Sam's voice broke. We reined to a halt, giving him time to work the trail away from there.

Behind us, the top edge of a red moon lifted above the rim of the world, throwing a faint light on the wagon and on a drying rack standing close by.

The rack had been built of mesquite poles set upright into the ground. A few short strips of buffalo meat, out of reach of the wolves and other varmints, still hung from the high crossbars.

Uncle Pack rode under the rack and lifted down strips of meat. He bundled the strips and hung them to his saddle horn, like the Indians had done.

"Just in case we git lank where it ain't safe to shoot meat," he explained.

I stared at the dark shapes of the wagon and drying rack, thinking what a lonely, solitary thing a wagon camp could be, resting there under the pale stars, without men or mules to give it life.

I thought some about the murdered hide hunters who lay scattered about somewhere in the grass. I couldn't see them and didn't want to. Once they had been men. Now, they were no different from the buffalo they had slaughtered around the wallow—fit only for the wolves and the buzzards to feed on.

Somehow, the thought didn't bother me. Maybe it was because I'd never known them. Maybe it was because of what Sanderson had said about hide hunters. Mostly, I think, it was because somewhere along this trip, I had come to see a thing that had always been right under my nose, yet I'd never paid any mind to it before. That is, how close life is tied up with death, so that you can't have one without the other. Everything on earth kills to live, then turns around and gets killed, so that something else can live. That was the pattern. I could see it now, and I guessed there wasn't a thing, from a man to a tumblebug, could change it.

Sam opened, and my thinking switched to Lisbeth and Little Arliss; and as I followed after Sam, I came to know another thing.

Maybe me and Lisbeth and Little Arliss and Papa and Mama and friends of ours, like Burn Sanderson, didn't amount to any more in this world than any other living creature. But like all the other creatures—like the buffalo, the screwworm, the prairie wolf, the high-flying goose, or the hole-digging gopher—our lives were important to us, and each of us would fight to keep them just as long as we could—and try to help those we loved to do the same.

Papa

## Eleven

I DON'T recollect much of the nightlong ride that followed. The soaking in the buffalo wallow had taken most of the bite out of my wounds and sunburned skin. That, topped off with a full stomach of good food, was too much. My bone-tired body relaxed. I slept in the saddle.

I'd heard old-timers tell about sleeping in the saddle and always figured it for brag talk, but that night I learned it could be done.

It was more dozing than real sleeping, I guess. For I do remember pieces and snatches of things. Like the bitterness in old man Searcy's voice when Papa and Sanderson tried again to talk him out of taking his turn at running.

"She's my grandgirl," he argued. "I got as much right to run myself to death trying to save her as ary one of you young bloods!"

Most of what I remember, though, wasn't talk. It was the steady squeak of saddle leather, the muffled drumbeat of horses' hoofs pounding the turf, and, above all, the never-failing trail cry of Savage Sam, calling us on across the shimmering silver of the moonlit grass.

It wasn't till Sam's voice faltered, then hushed altogether, that I started awake. I looked around. In the pearl-gray light of dawn I saw Burn Sanderson, some fifty yards ahead, reining his mount to a halt on the bank of a small creek. In the bed of the creek a trickle of water flowed between crumbling banks of brown sandstone. The water puddled in places, and the still surfaces of the puddles shone bright silver between a scattering of live oaks, willows, and cottonwoods.

Beyond the creek, the ground lifted like a great shaggy dew-wet blanket, rumpled and creased, sweeping up to high, flat-topped hills, purple in the distance. The upper edges of the hills glowed pink with the light of a rising sun we couldn't yet see.

We rode jaded horses toward Sanderson, with Papa calling out, "What have you found, Burn?"

Sanderson was slow to answer. "Not for sure yet," he finally said. "I'm just watching that dog."

Ahead, I could see Sam racing up one side of the creek, then down the other, darting this way and that between the trees, scrambling up the rock ledges, only to wheel and come splashing back through the water. He whimpered with eagerness, yet couldn't seem to straighten out the trail, and his hasseling was loud in the morning stillness.

Sanderson said at last, "Believe I'd call him in till we can scour around a little."

He touched spur to his horse and rode slowly down into the creek bed, searching the ground as he went. Papa whistled and called to Sam, who came racing toward him, looking excited. He must have thought Papa had located the scent he couldn't find; for when Papa stepped down and tied a rope around his neck, Sam tried to fight it for a minute, then gave up and stood, tail-tucked and droopy, whining like Papa had whipped him.

Ahead, Sanderson located something that caught his interest. He swung to the ground, squatted, and felt around over a bare patch of drift sand with his hands. As we rode up, he reached suddenly and lifted a buried bone out of the sand. It was a piece of rib bone, with shreds of gnawed meat still attached to one edge. A swarm of brown fire ants clung to the meat.

Sanderson rose from his squat and motioned with the bone.

"They buried their campfire here," he said. "Not more than an hour ago. And they left out in a hurry."

The men all peered down at the patch of clean sand.

"How you come by all that information?" Wiley Crup demanded.

Sanderson looked at Crup like he was tired of the sight of him. "The sand is still warm," he explained patiently. "And since it was wiped clean, not one living varmint's had time to make a track in it."

An ant stung his hand. He flung the bone aside and wiped crawling ants from one hand with the other.

"And if they hadn't quit this camp in a hurry," he added, "they'd never have left a piece of meat sticking out where the ants could get to it."

"You reckon they heard Sam?" Papa asked.

"You can depend on it," Sanderson said.

I remembered how quickly the Indians had broken camp that first morning when they heard Sam.

Sanderson climbed back into the saddle. He looked around at the men and nodded to Papa.

"We'll take a little *pasear,* Jim," he said. To the rest of us, he added, "Y'all strip the gear off the horses and cook up a batch of grub. We'll be back in time to help eat it."

"Why ain't we pushing on?" demanded Uncle Pack. "Ever' minute we lose gives them hostiles that much bigger lead."

"Trouble is, Uncle Pack, we don't know which way to push," Sanderson explained. "From the way that dog acts, I'd say they've split on us. Been expecting that to happen."

"We take the dog?" Papa asked.

"Let him rest," Sanderson said. "We'll need him worse later on."

Papa handed me the rope that Sam was tied to. Sanderson led off across the creek and Papa followed. They rode north at a jog trot toward the high hills. Both leaned low out of their saddles, combing the grass for signs. A mile or two out, they would separate and ride half-circles back into camp. That way, they could tell for sure if the Indians had split up.

106

I led Sam to a live oak and tied him to a drooping branch. I dismounted and, like the others, unsaddled my horse and removed the bridle. I stumbled down to the creek, where I drank and washed my face.

The horses drank, too, then hunted a sand bed to wallow in, which is a horse's way of washing up. They lay down on their sides and kicked and squirmed and raked their heads back and forth across the sand. They rolled over and did the same for the other side. They grunted with the pleasure of sanding off their sweat. Getting up, they spraddled themselves, shook the sand out of their hair, then moved on out to graze.

The men built a fire and started breakfast. Their movements were draggy. They fumbled at the simplest tasks. Most of what they had to say was soon said; after that, they kept the silence of men stupid with weariness and loss of sleep.

I guessed they were all worn to a frazzle. I know I was. I'd been on the go for so long, I couldn't hardly tell straight up from a good living. Now and then, I'd have a hard go of it just remembering where I was or what I was doing. I'd look at a tree or a rock or an old buffalo chip and have to study for a long time to lay the proper name to what I saw.

It wasn't the pain so much. That had eased off a good deal; and I'd pretty well gotten used to living with what was left. But the tiredness—it was a load nearly too heavy to pack around.

I caught myself standing and staring at Sam. After a spell, it came to me that he was whimpering and licking his feet. I guessed they were sore and something ought to be done about it. Let Sam wear out, and we'd be pretty well stringhalted.

I went to where Herb Haley was squatted over the fire, dropping chunked-up pieces of fat-back into a frying pan. I picked up a couple of chunks and took them over and started greasing Sam's feet. The thick, tough pads were worn off till they were paper thin, with the pink showing through. One pad had a bad cut across it and the cut oozed blood.

Back at the fire, I heard Lester White say, "This looks

like an excellent location for the horse ranch I have in mind."

"Some appearances," Uncle Pack said, "is deceiving."

"Possibly," White admitted. "But here is good water, fine grazing, a salubrious climate."

"Climate!" Uncle Pack snorted. "Man, this country's got no climate. All it's got is weather, and that comes whole-sale. Let a four-five year drouth hit, and it'd crowd a pack rat to find grass enough to line his nest."

"But the buffalo," White protested. "How can he exist under such conditions?"

"The buffler, he's smart," Uncle Pack said. "He drifts with the weather. Rain falls on the Rio Grande, he heads for it. Wet spell comes to Canady, he trails north."

I heard Bud Searcy call to me. I looked toward him. He hadn't moved from where he'd stripped the gear from his horse. He'd just dropped his saddle right there and now lay, using it for a pillow.

I went to stand over the old man. He lifted his canteen.

"Travis, my boy," he said in a quavery voice, "my canteen's dry. Would you kindly fill it for a pore old man?"

I knew that tone of voice. I remembered all the times he'd used it to take advantage of Lisbeth. It was, "Honey, will you do this?" and "Honey, will you fetch me that?" Always in that quavery, pore-mouth voice. And always for "yore pore old grandpappy." Running her half to death to keep up with his wants, while he lazed around in the shade, brag-talking and spitting his nasty tobacco juice all over the place.

Yesterday and last night, when he'd argued to take his turn at running, I'd been about ready to look up to Searcy a little, thinking maybe there was some man in him, after all. Now, I decided that all had been just show-off; he was the same old work-dodging windbag he'd always been.

I came close to telling him to go fetch his own water, that there were others around could use some rest. Then I took a second look. I saw how his blubber belly had shrunk, how his hands trembled, how gray his face was— like all the blood had been drained out. I saw how blue his lips were and what a look of defeat his watery old eyes held.

It came to me then that—for this time, at least—he wasn't just trying to use me. This time, he was in real need of help.

I took his canteen and walked upstream, past where the horses had muddied the water. I filled it and started back, taking a little different route, and came across a thing so curious that for a moment I forgot all about Searcy.

It was a pile of some forty or fifty horseshoes. Every shoe was bright with recent wear. And over the heap of shoes, lying in the form of a cross, was spread a couple of long narrow strips of torn blanket.

I stood and stared at my find, but couldn't make anything of it. I heard Searcy call out and took him his water. He set out to build me up, telling me what a fine upstanding young man I was to help a pore old man; but I didn't stay to listen. I hurried off to tell the men about my discovery.

On the way, I caught sight of Ben Todd. He stood, still as a mouse, watching something he'd found in a couple of catclaw bushes.

I halted. I looked to where he was looking. I saw wild morning glories blooming in the tops of the catclaw bushes. Their vines were spindly thin, but the pale, powder-blue flowers were as big as teacups.

Dipping and diving, darting from one flower to another, were two hummingbirds.

They were different from the hummingbirds that fed on Mama's flowers, back at home. Their nectar-sucking beaks were longer. Their black-green bodies were longer, too; or, at least, slimmer. And under their throats each wore a patch of pale yellow that somehow—when the light struck them at just the right angle—flashed red.

A stick popped under my boot, and the hummingbirds disappeared. Ben Todd turned, smiling shyly.

"Purty things, ain't they?" he said. "Ruby-throated hummingbirds, I think. Migrating south for the winter. Furtherest west I ever seen one."

I told Ben Todd about the pile of horseshoes. He called

to the others. We all went to see. Nobody had any more idea of its meaning than I did.

We were all standing around, still trying to puzzle it out, when Sanderson came riding in from downstream. We pointed to the pile of shoes. He nodded, like it was a common sight.

"Nearly always," he said, "an Injun will pull the shoes off any horse he steals."

"But why?" Herb Haley asked. "A smooth horse, he just goes lame all the quicker."

Sanderson shook his head. "I asked an old Tonk scout about it once. Best I could learn, the Injun figures if the Almighty meant for a horse to wear shoes, He'd have put 'em on his feet."

"But the crossed strips of blanket?" Herb Haley asked. "What do they mean?"

*"Quién sabe?"* Sanderson said. "Makes no more sense than wiping out signs of their campfire, then leaving this pile of horseshoes right out in the open, where they're bound to be seen."

He rode toward the campfire. We followed afoot. When we got there, I noticed Sam licking his feet again. I went to finish my greasing job and found that he had eaten the chunks of fat-back. So I got some more, greased his feet again, then watched him eat what was left of those chunks.

The men had started eating when I got back to the fire. I joined them and saw Papa come riding in from the west. Uncle Pack waved a hand toward the hills.

"What'd y'all find out yonder?"

"About what I expected," Sanderson said. "They've split up on us."

"How many ways?"

"I'll know in a minute."

We waited till Papa rode in, his face looking strained, his eyes sick with worry.

"How many trails did you locate," Sanderson asked.

"Two," Papa said. "One heading west along this draw. The other'n leading back to the southwest."

"That makes three, then," Sanderson said.

Papa swung down from his saddle and squatted to eat.

Uncle Pack shook his head, frowning. "The question is, which trail do we foller?"

"We'll have to leave that to Sam," Sanderson said.

"But how is the dog to know?" Lester White inquired. He frowned, studying for a moment, then went on. "He trails by scent. When the boy is on the ground, the dog can smell him. But once the boy is mounted, where is the scent? It can't hang in the air for long in this wind. Which means that all the dog has left to follow is the scent of the horses. And now, with the horses separated into three groups, it seems inconceivable that the dog can know which group to follow."

My heart sank. I never had thought of it in that light before.

I looked to Sanderson for help, but found no real comfort in the thoughtful look on his face.

He shook his head. "You've got a real poser there, Mr. White," he said. "But the way I see it, you're overlooking one thing. When it comes to sifting scent, a dog with a good nose has got powers outside the reach of a man's understanding."

"It's like what tells a honker goose spring's broke at his nesting grounds in Canada," Ben Todd said. "Man can't explain it, but the goose knows. So he quits Texas and heads north."

"That's putting a lot of trust in a dog," White said.

"Right now," Sanderson said bleakly, "a dog's all we got left to put any trust in."

*Apache*

## Twelve

WE had to catch and saddle Searcy's hors
for him, then help him into the saddle. H
made a show of trying to pass it off as nothing mucl

"Jest a mite stiff in the j'ints," he said. "Old hoss don
travel like a colt no more. But it'll pass off."

He stiffened his back and lifted the slump out of h
shoulders. But I couldn't help noticing that the skin of h
face was still a pasty white and the hands holding h
shotgun were mighty shaky.

When I went to untie Sam, I found him almost as f;
gone as Searcy. And Sam made no bones about his mi
eries. It took him a second try to get to his feet, and the
he could hardly walk. Every time he set a foot down,
was like he expected to step in hot ashes.

Worry must have showed in my face, for Sandersc
told me, "He'll loosen up, once he takes the trail again.

He touched spur to his horse and rode up close.

"But boost him up across my saddle for now," he adde
"Won't hurt to save his old feet when we can."

I picked up Sam by his slack back hide and swung hir
up across Sanderson's lap. There he lay, belly down, wit
Sanderson holding him on, while we rode better than
mile to where Papa had found a trail of horse track
leading to the southwest.

Sam would have nothing to do with this trail. We set him down in the middle of the tracks and whistled him out. He crippled around for a while, smelling here and there, made one wide circle, then came back to sit on his tail and look up at Sanderson, whimpering and whining. He made it plain that all he was interested in here was another ride.

Papa got down and handed him up to Sanderson, then he rode north toward the second trail, the one following west up the creek.

It was the same thing there. The tracks of the horses were plain in a sand bar that the creek had thrown up in flood time; but Sam wouldn't trail them. He didn't spend more than a couple of minutes nosing around over the trail before he was back, looking up at Sanderson, begging for another ride.

When he got it, Wiley Crup, who was on foot now, snorted in disgust. "Now I've seen it all," he said. "Pothounds let to ride, while good men are made to run!"

Sanderson shook his head slowly. "Wiley," he said, "there's times when a good pot-hound can be worth more than a dozen men."

We rode east, with hatbrims pulled low against the light of the rising sun. We traveled spread out, with every man cutting for sign of the horse trail leading north toward the high, far-off hills that were now changing from purple to blue. We rode till Sanderson began to look bothered, evidently thinking we'd overridden the trail.

Then Sam, who'd been grunting his pleasure at getting to ride, cut loose with a shrill yelp. It came so sudden that it spooked Sanderson's horse. Then Sam let out a bawl and went to clawing for footholds against the polished saddle leather.

Quickly, Sanderson cupped a hand under Sam's rump and heaved him out of his lap. Sam hit the ground and went charging through the grass. A second later, without even bothering to wring his stump tail, he opened, whimpered a time or two, and opened again. Then he took off running, nose to the ground, lined out toward the hills, the rise and fall of his high-pitched trail cry coming back to us clear and regular.

Ben Todd slapped his leg. "He's got it!" he shouted. "The son-of-a-gun!"

Lester White was plainly impressed.

"He's a caution, all right!" Uncle Pack said. "Stacking the landscape behind him like a dog what's been laid up and rested for a week!"

I didn't say a word about Sam's finding the trail. Papa didn't either. But I could see the relief on his face, and I guessed he was as choked-up proud of Sam as I was.

So we took up the chase again, the man-killing, horse-killing, dog-killing grind that wore on and on.

It wasn't speed so much that beat us down; Sam wasn't that fast on trail. It was just the steady going, with never a letup for a real rest. It was the awful distances we had to cover. And, worst of all for me, it was the nagging dread that when we caught up with the Indians, we might be too late.

Who was to protect Lisbeth from Broken Nose? And Little Arliss. With that hair-trigger temper of his, he was bound to tangle with Gotch Ear again.

We kept driving toward the hills, and the hills kept moving away. The jaded horses jogtrotted with heads held low, snuffing and blowing. The men rode slumped in their saddles, silent for the most part, with the turnover of those who traveled afoot coming more often now.

I wondered how Sam could hold up for so long. His feet were worn clear down to the quick. If they weren't bleeding now, they would be before the day was over. Yet he still kept driving, as strong and steady as ever.

The grass thinned to scattered bunches, finally played out altogether. Now we moved across country that was all hummocky blow-sand. The sand was a grayish pink and lay there in the prairie like a huge lake, with the hummocks and drift mounds looking like waves on water.

The strip we crossed, maybe a mile wide, was nothing more than a narrow finger of this great lake of sand. Looking to the west, I could see it reaching on out, as far as the eye was good.

It was while riding across the sand that I took notice of how many creatures were on the move—all sorts of snakes, gray lizards, huge black tarantulas, and terrapins.

As we entered the grass again, I rode past the trash-littered mound of a red-ant bed and looked down on it. Narrow lanes led away from the hole in several directions, and along these lanes the ants raced frantically back and forth.

I knew then what was fixing to take place. Before I could mention it, Ben Todd, riding close by, spoke up in an anxious voice.

"It's coming on to rain," he said.

"Rain!" Herb Haley said, surprised. He looked up and all around. "Why, they ain't a cloud in sight."

"But yonder," said Ben Todd, "goes a bunch of doves heading for a roost—here in the middle of the morning."

I glanced up. The doves, dark against a milky white sky, went hurtling past, making little whistling noises.

"And down here," Sanderson added, pointing, "is an alligator turtle on the prowl. Catch one of them old boys this far off from water, and rain is a dead certainty."

The turtle was a big ugly rascal, with a shell ridged down the middle. His tail was nearly a foot long, and so was his thick neck. He had a head on him the size of your fist, and there was no fear in him. He rose on his short bowed legs, lifting his head and tail clear of the ground, and glared at us. He blew at us like a mad snake. He made it plain that he was ready to take on all comers.

As we slogged on, following the steady ring of Sam's voice, the air got heavy and hard to breathe. The grass stood dead still and silent. A thickening haze all but smothered the high hills that had stood out so bright and sharp-edged at daylight. More doves passed over, flying at top speed. Now and then, too far out for us to have disturbed them, great flocks of little gray birds would rise suddenly up out of the grass. They'd take off in a low, jittery flight, barely skimming the top of the grass, wheel, and maybe go right back to light down where they came from.

When the clouds came, they were big thunderheads, one beside the other, piling up back of the hills. Their ragged white edges lifted above the flat-topped ridges, giving them shape and color again.

We rode toward them, watching them stack up higher

and higher, till finally we could see their dark centers, churning and tumbling with threat.

Little wind puffs began sneaking up from behind. For a cooling moment, one would tug hard at our sweaty clothes before racing on toward the storm; and you could mark its course by the grass bowing before it.

Gradually, the wind puffs came more often and cut wider swaths across the grass. They mounted in strength till they became great surges in a steady wind that pulled toward the storm. The increasing roar of the wind all but drowned out the sound of Sam's trail cry.

The trail led past a buffalo wallow. It was a big one, filling a swag that lay off to our right. In it, come to take comfort from the stifling heat, were some twenty buffalo—cows, calves, and a couple of bulls. Now, one by one, the buffalo lumbered to their feet. They stood in the wallow, with heads lifted, while muddy water streamed from their coarse black hair.

They had to have heard us, yet it wasn't us that had disturbed them and it wasn't us they were concerned with. If one ever looked our way, I never saw it. All stood with raised muzzles pointing toward the storm. When at last they began straggling out of the wallow, led by one old bull, it was toward the storm they moved.

The high-climbing front lifted higher. All the clouds became one. It reached out to spread over us and hide the sun. The underbelly of the cloud glowed yellow-green. Sight of that strange light touched some sense of warning far back in my mind. Great crooked fingers of lightning clawed suddenly across the face of the cloud and thunder shook the hills.

For a second, I felt the big lift of spirit that, for me, such storms always brought. Then, knowing how quickly a heavy rain could wipe out the trail scent that Sam followed, dread took over, and I rode toward the storm hating the very sight of it.

We came to the foot of the hills, where the land slanted sharply up. Here, the smooth rolling plain gave way to rounded ridges snaking down from the hills like the brace roots of great trees. Dividing the ridges were dry water courses, ranging in size from small crooked gullies to great cut-bank draws with walls of bare earth standing twenty feet high.

The trail led Sam along the hump of a ridge. We followed him, watching the play of lightning deep inside the black cloud, listening to the boom and roll of thunder among the hills. Then, almost at once, the wild wind driving hard at our backs shut down, leaving us to ride in a dead calm. Nothing stirred, not even a blade of grass, and I got the feeling that every creature on the face of the earth, besides us, had found itself a hiding place, where it lay, hushed and waiting.

That's when we heard it—a sullen, mounting, hammering roar that smothered Sam's voice, that all but drowned out the thunderclaps themselves.

I knew then what the threat was I'd missed back there when I'd first noticed that strange glow of yellow-green light in the cloud.

My voice cracked with fear when I cried out, "That's hail!"

"Go catch the dog!" Sanderson yelled at me, then called sharply to the others. "The balance of you scatter and hunt for cover!"

Sam wasn't more than a hundred yards ahead; but I don't believe I'd have ever caught him in time. He seemed to be driving harder than ever, like maybe the trail was the hottest he'd ever smelled it. Also, my horse was too jaded.

Then Papa came spurring past on a horse that still had some bottom left. Gradually, Papa gained on Sam, finally caught up with him.

"Hold it, Sam!" I heard him call. "That's enough, now. Hold it, boy!"

But Sam kept driving on, his voice faint against the roar of the oncoming hailstorm.

Papa spurred up and cut in front of Sam and yelled at him again. When Sam dodged around the horse, Papa downed his catch rope. He reached out and laid his loop on Sam like he would a wild hog, yanking it shut across Sam's shoulders and between his forelegs.

Sam yelped and struggled frantically, as Papa lifted him into the saddle. There, he tried to kick loose, then snarled and snapped at Papa. Papa boxed his jaws and scolded him, and after that, Sam gave up and lay still, whimpering and whining.

With Sam caught, I quit quirting my horse. Right away, he came to a full stop and I could feel the trembling weakness of him between my legs. As Papa rode back toward me, I looked past him toward the white wall of rain and hail beginning to fill a slot in the hills. It wasn't more than half a mile off, and coming fast, with a fearful roar.

Back of me, I heard somebody shout. Papa lifted a hand, pointing.

"Looks like Ben Todd's located something," he yelled.

I swung my horse around to ride beside Papa. Across a wide ravine, Ben Todd sat his horse on a high hump of ground, calling and motioning with his hat.

We rode toward him. From all around, I could see other members of the party riding up out of the draws and across folded ridges, headed toward Ben.

"It ain't much of a place," Todd said when we reached him. "But it'll shelter us for a while."

"That'll beat anything I found," Burn Sanderson said. "Lead off. We ain't got much time."

Todd led off, and the rest of us straggled after him. We struck an old buffalo trail and followed it, riding single file toward a break in the rim of a wide canyon that led down out of the hills. The trampling hoofs of thousands of buffalo, following this same trail for thousands of years, had cut it deep into the soil. It was so deep and narrow that in places we had to lift our feet out of the stirrups and hold them high to give the horses room to squeeze through.

We nearly didn't make it in time. A shrieking wind racing ahead of the storm, hit while we were still in the open. It struck with a jolt that staggered some of the horses and snatched the breath out of my mouth. Then we dropped down into the canyon, where the high wall broke the force of the wind but didn't hold off the first scatter of rain and hail.

The raindrops were icy cold against our backs. Some of the hailstones were big as taw marbles and bounced when they hit the ground. One caught me about the bur of one ear with all the jar and sting of a rifle ball.

Sam let out a startled yelp, and I knew that he'd been hit, too.

We hurried faster along the rock-littered bed of the dry watercourse. We whipped around a tight bend and pulled to a halt under the shelter that Ben Todd had located.

To me, holding a hand to my aching jaw and seeing more and bigger hailstones falling outside, Todd's shelter seemed perfect. It was a high clay bank, deeply undercut by flood water. It shelved out over us like a roof. No rain or hail could touch us here, and there was room to spare, for both horses and men.

"The only thing," Sanderson said as we swung to the ground, "is how long can we stay?"

"I said it wasn't much of a place," Todd said. "But it was all I could find."

Sanderson said quickly, "I didn't mean it as a complaint, Ben."

Todd nodded. "I didn't take it you did. But I'll allow it could turn into a trap."

"That sure ain't no lie," Wiley Crup said. "Me, I've seen floodwater with six- and eight-foot fronts come charging down draws like this, kicking up more dust than a runaway mule team."

He looked around like maybe he'd seen a lot of important sights nobody else had.

"Every man and horse in this outfit could git drowned here," he added. "Was enough water to fall fast enough."

Sanderson spoke with an edge to his voice. "You find a better place, Wiley?"

About then, the full force of the storm hit; and the hammering roar of it and the wreckage it brought on was enough to hold us all silent.

The first hailstones were piddling compared to what fell now. Out of the roaring blackness above rained ice balls bigger than your fist. They'd hit the ground and bounce three feet high, then get busted wide open by the first chunk of ice that struck them.

Across the draw from us, the ground sloped up to prairie level. The slope was overgrown with tall grass.

Huddled up under the protecting ground shelf, we watched in awe as the rain of ice chunks beat the grass to the ground, chopped it up, drove it into the earth, then overlaid the whole mess with a litter of shattered ice.

I thought of Lisbeth and Little Arliss, and a shiver shook me.

I looked around for Papa. He was squatted on his spurs. He had his elbows propped on his knees, his chin cupped in his hands. And he was crying.

It wasn't out-loud crying. But his face was all torn up, tears ran down his cheeks, and while I looked, his body jerked with a spasm that I knew came from a deep inside sob with the lid clamped on.

I felt again the great emptiness that I'd known back there before Sam caught up with me at the water hole. If Papa had lost all hope, I guessed we'd come to the end of our string.

Burn Sanderson moved quickly to lay an arm across Papa's shoulders. He gave Papa a rough shake.

"Here, now," he said. "Get a grip on yourself, Jim." He had to shout to be heard above the roar of the pounding hail. "We ain't near done yet."

Papa glanced at Sanderson, then away. He waved hand toward the pounding hail and said hopelessly, "Nothing can take battering like that and come out of it alive. Not even a horse, if he gets hit on the head!"

"Now, hold on," Sanderson shouted. "Don't you never think for a minute them redskins didn't find shelter. We did, and they're a heap wilder and more knowing of the country than us."

Before Sanderson finished speaking, the hail quit like it had been chopped off. Rain still poured down in driving sheets, but after the awful racket of that falling hail, what noise the rain made seemed like a whisper.

"But the trail," Papa said. "It's been wiped out. We got nothing left to foller."

Sanderson studied on that for a minute, then said, "But we still got a direction, Jim. And we still got Sam. We foller the direction long enough, and Sam'll pick us up a trail."

Beside me, Wiley Crup raised a protest. "But that coul

take days!" he said. "With all the country we'd have to scour, trying to locate a trail."

Sanderson nodded. "It sure could," he said.

Crup stared at Sanderson like he thought he was out of his head. Then he stabbed a finger toward the tired horses that stood humped under their saddles.

"Just how much longer do you expect them dead-beat horses to hold out?" he demanded.

"Till they go down," Sanderson said.

"Then what?"

"Then we take it afoot."

Crup exploded. "You expect a man to ride his horse this far from home, then walk back?" he asked.

Sanderson said in a flat tone of voice, "You got any ideas about going back right away, you'll walk, anyhow. We're short of horses."

Crup stiffened. "You'd try to take my horse?"

"I mean we'll *take* it," Sanderson said.

Crup stared hard at Sanderson. With a casual movement, he shifted his heavy rifle to his left shoulder. Then, so quick it didn't seem like he'd moved, he had a six-shooter in his right hand, pointed straight at Sanderson. He bared his squirrel teeth and sneered, "What makes you think you can git away with that?"

Sanderson looked past Crup's gun like it wasn't there. He grinned and gave his head a sideways nod.

"One thing," he said, "is the direction Bud Searcy's got his scatter-gun pointed."

Crup started and looked around. I did the same. Old man Searcy sat with his back braced against the clay wall. He held his shotgun pointed at Wiley Crup.

"You turn one hair, Wiley Crup," he warned, "and I won't leave enough of you to scrape up with a hoe!"

The gun muzzle wobbled in his hands. Like always, there was too much brag and bluster in his voice. But the glassy shine in his eyes convinced me. If Wiley Crup was looking for a chance to get blown into scrapmeat, he'd looked far enough.

Evidently, Crup saw it the same way. He let his six-shooter sag. He took a couple of steps backward, saw other guns being drawn, and froze.

He didn't say anything, and nobody else did.

Back of him the rain began to slack off. Around the bend of the draw swept a curling front of floodwater, pushing ahead of it a lot of trash and dirty brown foam. It lacked a good deal of being the horse-drowning flood Crup had predicted, maybe because too much water was locked up in ice. But it was enough to make Papa and Sanderson and Searcy get to their feet. Otherwise, nobody paid any attention to the water. They just stood waiting on Crup.

After a while, Crup swallowed and said grudgingly, "I reckon I was out of line."

"That's how we got it figured," Uncle Pack said.

Crup took a second look at the drawn guns and accusing stares. He sucked in a quick breath and terror showed in his face.

"But you ain't cutting me out of the bunch!" he cried. "Not way out here, clear to the backside of nowhere!"

"That's up to Sanderson," Uncle Pack said. "Don't make me no never-mind, one way or t'other."

Crup turned to face Sanderson. "Sanderson!" he begged. "You can't do it! Not *afoot*. Them siwashes—they'd lift my hair before sunset!"

Sanderson stood frowning down at a dead pack rat floating past on the muddy water swirling around his feet. The icy water was rising and beginning to fill my boots. I heard Sam whine, saw him wading stiffly toward higher ground. The cold water made some of the horses nervous. They snorted and stomped around.

I wished the men would hush arguing. I wished they'd set Wiley Crup afoot, shoot him, or do something. I couldn't stand much more of this. I was shaking all over.

Finally, Sanderson lifted his head. "Way I see it," he said, "Wiley's still another gun. Best shot in the bunch, too. And once we overhaul them Injuns, any extra gun won't be none too many."

He turned toward his horse. "Now," he said, "let's clear out of this draw before we get drowned out."

*Travis*

## Thirteen

WE boosted Searcy back into the saddle. I waded out to where Sam stood shivering and handed him up to Papa. Papa held him in his saddle and looked toward Crup.

"Wiley," he said, "I'll give you a piece of advice. Don't pull a gun on Sanderson again. If he don't kill you, I will."

It gave me a lift to hear Papa talk like that. The tone of his voice told me that he had got hold of himself, that he was ready to push on again.

We rode out into the tail-end leavings of the storm that boomed and roared as it rolled on toward the south. What rain fell now was thin and drizzly, but still enough to wet us.

We came to the break in the canyon wall. We found the buffalo trail a foot-deep millrace of yellow water, loaded heavy with trash and tumbling chunks of white ice. It didn't look like much of a way out, but it was the only one, so we took it.

The horses slipped and floundered, scrambling for footholds against the slippery trail bottom. They snorted and stomped at the icy water dragging against their legs. They grunted and strained and were badly winded by the time they'd brought us out on top.

There, we reined them to a halt, giving them a breather while we gazed out on a bleak and disheartening sight. In every direction, as far as the eye could reach, white balls and chunks of ice covered the ground. Where thirty minutes ago we'd ridden through grass that stood stirrup high, now a cow couldn't have picked a bellyful of graze off a thousand acres.

For all a body could tell, this might have been in the dead of winter. What little breeze trailed after the storm had all the feel of winter. Moving across miles of ice, it picked up the cold of it, and the cold reddened our hands and faces and drove through our wet clothes, chilling our whole bodies. We shivered and our horses shivered and our breaths fogged white in the air.

Cold like this, coming so soon after we'd all been so sweaty hot, was hard to bear.

Sanderson blew on his hands. He said he didn't guess we'd get any warmer sitting there, so we moved out toward the gap in the hills that Sam had been headed for when we pulled him off the trail.

The ice crunched under the horses' feet. The cold drove deeper till I could feel the ache of it in my bones. My teeth went to chattering.

I glanced around at the others. They all looked as cold and miserable as I felt. Especially old man Searcy. He rode behind and a little off to the right of Wiley Crup, and the cold had him shaking till it looked like he might drop his shotgun any minute.

The shotgun, I noticed, was kept pointed in the general direction of Wiley's back.

After a while, that fact came to Crup's attention. I saw him cast a couple of wary glances back over one shoulder, then gradually sidle his horse toward the edge of the bunch.

Searcy sidled with him.

Crup, trying to act casual about it, shifted toward the other side. Just as casually, Searcy shifted with him.

There was no doubt left in Crup's mind now. He twisted in his saddle.

"Old man," he said angrily, "you got no call to keep pointing that scatter-gun at me."

Searcy presssed forked fingers against his lips and tried to spit through the fork, but he was so shaky with cold that most of the tobacco juice spattered down over his shirt front.

"Maybe not," he said to Crup. "But that's what I aim to keep doing."

Crup looked around at the others like he expected sympathy, but all he got was a couple of wry grins.

We rode on, past a dead coyote lying half buried in the ice; and after that, I saw all sorts of small creatures that had been beaten to death by the hail.

We passed a lone three-pronged live oak that grew beside a gully. The hail had stripped it. There wasn't a branch smaller than your arm left on it. The stub ends of the broken branches were split and shredded and had all the bark knocked off on the north side. It would take a long time for that tree to grow another top—if it lived.

I had to believe what Sanderson had said: that the Indians were bound to have located cover.

At last, we came to a high saddle between two hills. Here, Sanderson pulled up to make a study of the country that lay ahead.

I took a look at it, myself, but didn't see much. Just more flat-topped hills, separated by wide, sweeping valleys. The valleys were cut up some by deep ravines and old buffalo trails. These now ran full with flood water. The only hopeful thing I saw lay to the north, where the overcast of storm clouds was lifting, leaving a clear blue sky and the promise of warm sunshine.

The way my bones ached with cold, I could sure make good use of some sunshine.

Sanderson lifted a hand, pointing. He said, "See that main buffalo trail, leading to the northwest? I figure that's the route they took. Buffalo always pick the easy ground and the redskin knows it. Crowd him, and watch how quick he'll take to a buffalo trail for fast traveling."

Pack Underwood said, "You think we was crowding 'em? Back before the hail hit?"

"That's the way I read the sign," Sanderson said.

He paused, his keen eyes searching again the ice-littered hills and valleys.

"We'll foller that main buffalo trail," he said. "We'll spread out as far apart as we can see each other. That way, with everybody keeping his eyes skinned, somebody ought to cut their sign."

"What if we jump 'em?" Ben Todd wanted to know. "Sudden and accidental, I mean."

"However we jump 'em," Sanderson said, "we try first to cut 'em away from their main horse herd. We do that, we can handle 'em. We miss, and they'll blow out our lamps while we're still shooting horses from under 'em."

We spread out and rode forward in a mile-wide front. That is, all but Bud Searcy. He wouldn't spread out at all. He just dogged Wiley Crup's heels, with his shotgun held ready.

I heard Sam's eager yelp when he first caught the scent. I looked toward Papa and saw him boost Sam out of the saddle. Sam yelped again—this time in pain—when his sore feet hit the ice. Then he was circling, nose to the ground, and I heard the strain in Papa's voice as he urged Sam on.

"Git after it, boy," he said. "It's up to you, now!"

I reined to a halt and sat watching, listening, hoping.

Then Sam opened. He opened again; and if there'd been any doubt the first time, it was gone now. The ring of his voice was too sure-for-certain.

My heart swelled near to bursting.

Sam headed south, the regular rise and fall of his voice high-pitched and steady. I followed, hearing the excited shouts of the men and the pounding crunch of their horses' hoofs on the ice as they gathered in.

Uncle Pack called from a long way off. "You think he's got it?"

"I *know* he's got it," Sanderson shouted back.

I rode, wondering if it was pure accident that the Indians had cut square across the route Sanderson had expected them to follow; or was it a thought-up trick, calculated to throw us off track?

The trail led up a long slope, over a high hump, and down a steeper slant on the other side. Here, Sam swung right, trailing west, with loose ice clinking under his feet. I rode all alert and with a mounting sense of excitement, knowing that any trail on top of the ice had to be a fresh one, which meant we just might jump us some Indians any minute.

The overcast of clouds peeled back. A hot sun bore down, bringing comfort to our bone-chilled bodies.

It also set fire to the ice. Every chunk glinted and sparkled with such dazzling brightness that it all but blinded us. We rode now with tears blurring everything, following Sam more by ear than by sight.

I didn't like this, even a little bit. How could a body draw a bead on an Indian when he couldn't even see his gunsights? I worried with this for a couple of miles, then heard Uncle Pack grunt with relief.

"Be dog, if that ain't a sight for sore eyes," he said.

I wiped away my tears and looked ahead. Uncle Pack had sure told the truth. We'd come to the edge of the ice. Out front, not fifty yards away, stood tall grass again. The green of that grass was sure restful to the eye; and right then, looking out on the great sweep of it, I thought I'd never seen a prettier sight in my life. Even the smell of it was good.

Just before we rode into it, however, I glanced down and saw a thing that put a damper on my good feelings. It was a smear of blood in one of the tracks that Sam had left in the melting ice.

But if worn and bloody feet slowed Sam, I couldn't tell it. He set and held a pace that kept us jogging through the grass at a fast clip, forcing us to change often with whichever man ran on foot. The sun soon broke out the sweat on men and horses, but after that ride across the ice, nobody complained about sweating.

The trail led deeper and deeper into the rain-soaked hills. Some hills were big and some little, but each stood at the same flat-topped level, like they'd all been sliced off with one stroke of a big knife. A scattering of brush grew on some hills, and some didn't have any, but wind-rippled grass lay over them all.

Always, ahead of us, the hills seemed to lap and fold, one into the other, so that it never looked like there was an opening in between. Yet, before we ever got anywhere near a place that was solid, the hills seemed to move apart, leaving room for us to follow Sam through a valley that might be as much as a mile wide.

We crossed a buffalo trail and in the muddy bottom of it I saw blood in Sam's tracks again. Further along, we scared up a big band of antelope that swept across the trail in a blur of speed. Their scent muddled the trail for Sam and he had to circle several times before he could get lined out again. We rode up on him while he circled; and I saw him packing one forefoot and now and then lifting the offside hind one, so that part of the time, he ran on two feet only.

Then he opened, set all four feet to the ground, and was gone again.

It was along in the middle of the afternoon when the warning came.

There was nothing sudden about it, nothing the others could take note of. But it was strong enough to wake me out of the drooping, head-nodding doze I rode in. It put me on the alert again.

A slight but steady breeze blew out of the west, bringing Sam's voice straight back to us, loud and clear. But now there was a difference in the pitch of that voice. It was such a hair-thin difference that nobody who hadn't trailed varmints with Sam would have caught it, but I did—that little extra drive, a shade more urgency, a keener, wilder lift to the ring of it.

I knew what that meant, and the knowing of it tightened every nerve in my body. I crowded my horse up alongside Burn Sanderson, who rode with Papa and Lester White.

"Mr. Sanderson," I told him, "we're getting close!"

Sanderson stiffened. He gave me a quick look, then motioned for the others to pull in closer.

"You sure, boy?" he asked.

"Yes, sir," I said. "I'm *real* sure."

He reined to a halt. He made a quick search of the hill slopes on either side and of the long valley stretching out ahead of us. Papa and White did the same.

"But they ain't a thing in sight," Herb Haley said.

"The boy ought to could tell," Searcy said. "Was it my trail hound, I could tell in a minute."

Wiley Crup edged his horse away from Searcy. Searcy as quick to swing his shotgun around to cover him.

"Wiley, you hold still," he ordered. "I'm a feeble old an, but I ain't too feeble to press a shotgun trigger."

Wiley glared his hate at the old man, but he held still.

I felt desperate. Sam was closing in on the Indians. e might jump them any minute. And here we sat.

"Confound it!" I flared. "I tell you, Sam's moving in 1 them. Right now!"

"If we're that close," Sanderson said, "they're bound 've pulled off into some side valley. Maybe to get meat."

He sized up the bunch and nodded to Ben Todd. "Ben," : said, "you got a sharp eye. You and Mr. White, y'all ke to the high ground on the right. Me 'n' Travis here, e'll go left. Jim, you and the others catch up with that g. And stay caught up. Tromp on his heels if you have , but be in gun range when he leads you to them Injuns."

He reined his horse to the left, then added, "And member. The main thing is to cut 'em away from their ose horses."

He touched spur to his horse and rode, quartering left a long slant toward a dip between two hills. I went with m. Out of the tail of my eye, I could see Ben Todd and ester White riding at about the same angle toward the pposite hills. In the valley between, Papa and the others ashed their jaded horses to the limit, trying to overtake m.

I wondered if they ever could; for by now, anybody could ll that Sam was stepping up the pace. His voice was much ener, the beat of it much quicker. There was no longer y noticeable rise and fall to it. Now, it came to us in just le long quavering peal of sound, so wild and with so much ive that it stretched my nerve strings right up to the eaking point.

Maybe Sam's voice tore at Sanderson like it did at me; maybe Sanderson sensed the strain I was under. Any-w, he spoke up in time to keep me from going to pieces.

"Travis," he said, "when this show opens, it'll open fast. em Injuns, they're not going to wait around for you to nsider if it's best to do this or to do that. So the thing is,

129

get your mind made up first, then keep it made up. Yo
understand?" .

I said, "Yes, sir," and waited to hear more.

"Good," he said. "Now, what we've come for is to k
Injuns. It's the only way we can save Lisbeth and Lit
Arliss. No matter what unexpected thing crops up duri
the fight, that's what you want to keep in mind. K
Injuns."

"Yes, sir," I said.

He rode silent for a moment, then went on. "Headi
into a fight," he said, "all you can depend on for sure is th
you're going in scared."

I looked at him in surprise. I'd never thought of him
being scared of anything. As if he could read my though
he grinned and licked lips as dry as mine.

"Man or boy," he said, "it's all the same."

The last hundred yards of ground we covered was plen
steep. Footing for the horses was bad here. Either the
hoofs slipped on firm ground or sank hock deep into slop
mud. They bowed their backs and grunted with the stra
of the climb.

I glanced back for a last look at the others. Ben To
and Lester White, they'd disappeared into some fold of t
landscape. The hump of hill to our right hid all of Papa
party except for the drag end. I could still see old m
Searcy dogging along after Wiley Crup.

I listened for Sam, but the wind direction was wro
now. I couldn't hear him any more.

*Comanche*

## Fourteen

WE finally reached the gap between the hills. Just before we got to where we could e over, Sanderson reined to a halt. He dragged his Winester from his scabbard and stepped to the ground.

"We belly crawl from here," he told me. "We want a od look-see at what's on the other side before we skyline rselves."

I got down with my rifle. We dropped looped bridle reins, ground-stake our horses. We left them to catch their nd while we went crawling through the grass.

I crawled close beside Sanderson. I watched how he did ings and tried my best to do the same. Any slip-up made re, Sanderson would have to make first.

We crawled quiet and easy across the narrow ridge. We me to where the ground dropped away on the far side. e peered out through the grass—and both froze.

Just under us, less than a hundred yards away, grazed me twenty head of horses. Among them was the big stud at Gotch Ear had tried to ride. Beyond the herd, holding e horses against the hillside, Bandy Legs sat on his saddle buffalo hide. He was staring straight at us.

It was probably a happen-so that he was looking our

way, for he didn't appear disturbed. But it sure proved how smart we'd been to play it so cautious. If we had come riding across that ridge, Bandy Legs would have spotted us for sure.

A sudden outburst of yips and yells made Bandy Legs swing around to look the other way. It caused us to inch forward to where we could see better. And what we saw set the blood to pounding my ears.

It was Lisbeth and Little Arliss.

They were down in the middle of a quarter-moon valley that, half a mile away, opened into the bigger one we'd just climbed out of. They sat their horses beside a shallow wash now flooded with runoff water from the hills. Arliss was still naked except for his buffalo headdress. Lisbeth's garments were so tattered, they made her look like a scarecrow.

Near them, strung along the wash, were five Indians. Two I recognized: the Comanche and Broken Nose. The Comanche stood on the ground, holding to the bridle rein of my horse, Blue. The others were mounted. All, including Lisbeth and Little Arliss, sat staring toward the upper end of the valley, watching something I couldn't see.

I could hear it, though. It was a chase of some sort. The muffled drumming of heavy hoofs pounded the turf, and I could hear the familiar screeches of red savages closing in for a kill. From the sound of it, the chase was moving down our side of the valley and ought to cross our line of vision any second.

I wondered what the Indians were after.

Beside me, Sanderson whispered, "Not a bad setup. Knock off this close one, and we ought to could drive a wedge between the horse herd and them others before they can reach it."

I'd been packing my bottled-up rage for too long. It'd been lying like a hot rock inside my rib cage from the first time I saw Lisbeth and Little Arliss yanked around by the hair of their heads. Now, I stared down at the cruel, paint-streaked face of Bandy Legs and knew a big hunger to kill.

I eased my rifle forward. "Now?" I whispered.

"No. Hold it!" Sanderson said quickly. "Give Sam time to lead your papa and his bunch into the mouth of the draw. We'll have 'em in a trap then."

That wasn't actually true. Stopper both pinched ends of the valley, and the Indians could still get out on either side. Yet, to do so, they'd have to climb steep slopes, which would slow their getaway and give us good open shooting. The main trouble, as I saw it, was the width of the valley in the middle. I didn't much think a rifle ball would carry that far.

I lay listening and watching, trying to hold down the thumping of my heart. There was a brass-cartridge taste in my mouth. My lips stayed dry, no matter how often I licked them. I kept thinking: *We've come to kill Indians. We've got to kill them to save Lisbeth and Little Arliss!*

The noisy chase came into sight. It was a herd of some twenty or thirty buffalo. They came stampeding down the valley with a couple of Apaches riding hard after them.

One of the Apaches was Gotch Ear, still wearing his big black hat. He and his partner yelled at the tops of their voices.

The buffalo looked too big and clumsy for fast travel; yet their lumbering gait covered the ground at a pace that had the Indian ponies stretched out for all they were worth to gain on them.

Sanderson shook his head, as if finding it hard to believe what he saw.

"Now, that's young bucks for you," he said under his breath. "Stopping to pull off a frolic like this, when they're bound to know we're right on their heels."

I nodded. I remembered how they'd stopped their wild getaway run to watch a snake swallow a rabbit.

The chase came about even with Lisbeth and Arliss and the others watching. Gotch Ear's partner, riding on the far side of the herd, moved up beside a running cow. Plumed lance lifted high, he raced with her for a moment, edging in closer. Then he struck, driving the lance deep into the cow's side. The stricken cow bawled and made a quick sideways lunge with her head. The Apache wheeled his horse out of danger as the cow went down.

This was a daring kill, judging from the whoops of the Indians looking on. But laid up against the show Gotch Ear had in mind, it didn't amount to shucks.

I watched Gotch Ear now, as he edged his hard-running

pony in beside a monster bull; and it came to me that he carried no lance or any other weapon I could see.

Then he made his leap. He quit his horse and landed astride the bull. I caught a glint of sunlight on polished steel and knew that Gotch Ear was making an even bigger bid for glory than when he'd tried to ride that killer stud.

He aimed to cut down this big bull buffalo with only a knife!

He caught up a fistful of hump hair to hold with; and the way he hung down off the side of that running bull and went to work with his knife was a sight to curl your hair.

"I'm going back for the horses," I heard Sanderson whisper. "This turkey shoot's fixing to open."

I was so taken with the daring of Gotch Ear's show that I hardly knew when Sanderson left. I watched Gotch Ear plunge the long blade of his knife, time and again, deep into the side of the running buffalo. He was reaching low, stabbing for the heart, but evidently missing it. Blood spewed bright red from each new wound as Gotch Ear yanked his knife free for another lick. The bull bellowed with the pain of his wounds, but stayed on his feet and kept right on running with the others.

Then, riding in over the pain bawling of the bull, the pounding of hoofs, and the whooping and yelping of the Indians, came a sound that brought me up sharp. It was the quavering high-pitched voice of Savage Sam, driving full cry on a hot trail.

I glanced toward the lower end of the valley. I couldn't see Sam for the tall grass, but I could see Papa and the others rounding a shoulder of the hill, moving up to meet Gotch Ear and the stampeding buffalo.

I wasn't the only one to hear Sam. Already, the delighted yelps of the spectator Indians had changed to sharp, barking shouts of alarm.

I glanced toward them. I saw the Comanche leap astride my horse, Blue. I saw the others wheel their mounts around and lay the lash to them, and to the horses on which Lizbeth and Little Arliss were mounted.

Then here they came in a dead run, headed straight for the horse herd.

I couldn't wait to ask Sanderson when to shoot. The time was now, and I knew it!

I brought my rifle butt up to my shoulder. Bandy Legs caught the movement out of the tail of his eye. He swung around, holding still for an instant, trying to locate what he'd seen, and that instant was too long.

My ball lifted him out of the saddle like he'd been jerked loose with a rope.

Behind me came the pound of running hoofs and Sanderson's voice.

"That's laying 'em in the groove, boy!" he shouted. "Now, mount up and foller me!"

I leaped to my feet. Sanderson came spurring toward me, leading my horse. He dropped the bridle reins as he tore past. I grabbed them up and went into the saddle without touching a stirrup and took out after Sanderson.

Sanderson was spurring and quirting his horse, shouting at him, goading him into a frantic run down a slant of ground so steep it didn't look like a horse could keep on his feet.

My shot and the scent of fresh blood had spooked the Indian herd. Now, horses were whistling and snorting and scattering in all directions. Several headed straight across the valley where it would be as easy for the Indians to reach them as it would be for us to cut them off.

It took all Sanderson could get out of his tired horse to drive between these horses and the Indians racing toward them.

My horse never got that far. He stepped into a hole, stuck his nose into the ground, and turned tail-end-over-appetite.

I'd been looking for something like that, and when I felt him coming over, I quit the saddle, throwing myself as far away as I could.

I landed standing up, but my falling horse struck me from behind and slammed me to the ground. The way he lay, with his head doubled back under him, told me that he'd never get up again.

I crawled up behind him and used his body for protection. I reloaded and laid the barrel of my rifle across his rump. I looked along the length of it toward the screeching pack that raced up hill toward Sanderson and the stampeding horse herd. I heard two whiplash reports from Sanderson's repeater rifle. I saw one of the running horses go down. His flying hoofs slapped down a rider who'd tried to leap free of him. That Indian didn't get up.

I held off shooting for a second. I was searching for a certain target. I wanted Broken Nose, the Apache I hated the worst.

But I couldn't find him. Like every other fight I'd seen the savages take part in, there wasn't a whole Indian in sight. Each rode hanging to the off side of his mount, leaving nothing to shoot at except a leg hooked across a horse's back and a rawhide shield held against the animal's neck.

But yonder rode Lisbeth, sitting straight up, with her long blond hair streaming in the wind. Close behind raced a blaze-faced sorrel that Broken Nose sometimes rode. I figured that sorrel to be the one I wanted and lined my sights up on him, leading him a few inches, since it was a quartering shot. I squeezed the trigger and cut him down.

It was Broken Nose, all right. He landed running, and worked fast reloading, hoping to get in a shot while he was still on the ground and in sight.

To my left, Sanderson's gun spoke again. At the same instant, I heard Little Arliss call out in a wild scream of joy. "Sam! Sam!"

My glance flicked toward him as he leaped free of a running horse, and deep inside me I cried, *Wait, Arliss! Wait!*

I saw Arliss hit the ground and take off through the grass. I saw, too, the hard-driven arrow that barely missed him and how it went skipping across the grass tops like some live scared thing.

If Arliss saw the arrow, he paid it no mind. He went racing along a buffalo trail behind Gotch Ear and the stampeded buffalo. He was going to meet Sam. He kept calling, as he ran, "Sam! Sam!"

Then there was no longer time to watch Arliss; for now I was reloaded, and yonder was Broken Nose, making flying leap for the back of another horse that came running past him.

He landed astride; and as I swung my rifle around to cover him, I saw him lift a foot and stomp at the Apache clinging to the off side of the horse. He was trying to kick that one loose; but either he made a miscalculation, or the other Apache dragged him off, for they both tumbled to the ground before I could shoot.

They were out of sight for a second. Then, up out of the grass they came, running side by side, straight away from me; and now it *was* like a turkey shoot, and I pulled down on Broken Nose, drawing a close bead on the center of his bare back, knowing in my own mind that I had him dead to rights, with no chance for a miss.

Yet, at the very instant I squeezed off—like maybe he could tell my shot was meant for him—Broken Nose whipped his fire-hardened shield around to cover his back. My ball struck it, making it boom like a drum. But the bulge of the shield deflected the ball, and the high, keening wail of it spending itself harmlessly out across the valley filled me with bitter disappointment.

I worked frantically at jacking an empty shell from the firing chamber and thumbing a loaded one back into its bed. I slapped shut the breech lock. I brought my rifle up to my shoulder. Then, before I could shoot, Sanderson's repeater rifle cut loose again and sent Broken Nose and the other Apache plunging head first into the grass and out of sight.

Whether or not either had been hit, I had no way of knowing and no time to find out. For now, above all the yelling and shooting and trampling of hoofs, there lifted a long drawn-out, blood-chilling screech that was too close.

The hair prickled the nape of my neck as I swung my rifle around and brought it to bear on the Comanche. He'd split off from the others and now rode straight at me, not fifty yards away. He lay low along the back of my horse, Blue, and rode with a long arrow set in a short bow and had the bowstring pulled clear back to his ear.

The bowstring twanged. I ducked low and heard the whistle of the arrow cut short as it drove into the soft earth just behind me.

I raised to make a quick try at catching the Comanche in my sights. But I wasn't quick enough. Already, he was down off the side of Blue and swinging him away at an angle that used Blue's body as a protection.

Blue was my horse, the first I'd ever owned. I was proud

of him; and it was a hurtful, sickening thing for me to plant a ball in his heart and watch him roll dead—the same as you'd knock over a chicken-thieving coyote.

What drove the hurt deeper was the sight of the Comanche landing free and unharmed, to go racing off down the slant with his cowtail ropes of hair whipping the grass tops behind him. There went a perfect target. If only my rifle still held the bullet that had killed Blue!

Then I thought: *You've got a six-shooter, you fool!*

So I jerked out the side gun and snapped off a quick shot that struck the left side of the Comanche and set him spinning, with arms outflung, so that his shield slipped off his arm and flew in one direction and his bow in another.

I shot again and missed; and before I could get off a third shot, the Comanche had melted into the grass.

I held ready for a second, watching close, hoping he would show again, but he didn't, and shouts and shots beyond pulled my attention away. I looked out across a valley alive with scared and scattering horses and saw Sanderson shoot one of them, then kill the Apache who flung himself free as the horse went down.

I took a quick look around. Best I could tell, that was the last mounted Indian. Now, the only loose horse still packing a rider was the one Lisbeth rode. He'd shied away from the gunfire, veering off to chase after a stud and several mares that had cut in behind Sanderson.

The stud led them toward the far side of the valley at a dead run. I watched them taking Lisbeth with them and wished she'd jump off, but guessed she was too scared to think what to do.

I tucked away the six-shooter and began reloading the rifle. As I worked, I watched Sanderson rein his horse around to follow after Lisbeth. Then he leaped suddenly to the ground and stood in a half-crouch while he brought his rifle to bear on some target further down the valley.

He fired as I swung around to look, then fired again; but both shots missed and changed nothing about the picture laid out before my eyes.

It was a sight to choke off my breath.

Here came Little Arliss, headed back along the same trail he'd followed when he went to meet Sam. He was running like a scared jackrabbit. Close behind and gaining raced Gotch Ear, clutching his long, bloody knife. Moving up fast behind Gotch Ear came Savage Sam, running silent now, bent on catching Gotch Ear before the Apache could overhaul Arliss. And, straggled out far behind, riding past the dead bull buffalo, came Papa and the others, spurring and quirting horses too dead-beat ever to catch up.

All this I caught at a glance and understood at once.

Gotch Ear's show-off kill of the bull buffalo had led him head-on into a trap. When finally the huge beast went down under his knife, the Apache had leaped clear, expecting applause for his daring act. Instead, he'd heard Sam and caught sight of Papa and the others coming straight for him. He'd wheeled to head back toward his companions, only to see them racing away, leaving him afoot.

But yonder, coming to meet Sam, was Little Arliss, who had helped to shame and disgrace him. So Gotch Ear had made for Arliss, bent on getting revenge. If a rifle ball didn't cut him down first, he aimed to sink his knife into the little scamp who'd eaten his ear.

It looked like he'd get to do it, too. Arliss had evidently been too close to Gotch Ear before he saw him and turned to flee. Sam was still too far behind the Indian. Sanderson had stopped shooting, and Papa and the others had never started. That's what rattled me so, I guess, watching the fast-running Gotch Ear drawing closer and closer to Arliss, knowing Sam could never catch him in time, and wondering why nobody would shoot.

Panic held such a strangle hold on me that I couldn't realize that the magazine of Sanderson's rifle might have run dry, forcing him to stop and reload, or that Papa and the others rode in such a direct line with the chase that they couldn't shoot at Gotch Ear without danger of killing Little Arliss.

Almost too late, I came to my senses and swung my own rifle around to line in on Gotch Ear.

It wasn't too long a shot, maybe a hundred and fifty yards, but time for making it was running short. The fleeing Arliss wasn't more than fifteen steps ahead of Gotch Ear when he hit the shallow water in the wash, stumbled and went down.

Now, though, I had my sights laid in on Gotch Ear, dead center, leading him by about a foot.

I squeezed off—and missed him completely.

But when Little Arliss came up out of that muddy water, he was clutching a rock in each hand—and he didn't miss.

The first rock, bigger than my fist, caught Gotch Ear at about the belly button. It didn't stop him, but it must have sunk deep and been a real jolter, judging from the way he was bent nearly double as he came up.

Then Arliss cut down on him with the second rock. He bounced that one off the side of Gotch Ear's head with a force that sent the black hat flying. This straightened Gotch Ear up some and addled him worse. It sent him reeling and stumbling on past Arliss, holding his head with one hand and his belly with the other.

Arliss bent quick and came up with a couple more rocks, but he never got to use them.

This was on account of Sam.

Sam came in, driving full tilt and roaring like a mad bull. He made a long leap, nailed Gotch Ear by the neck, and took him to the ground.

They landed in the water with a big splash. They rolled and wallowed and pitched and knocked muddy water all over Little Arliss. The black hat floated off down the draw. Arliss stood away from the fight, holding a rock drawn back and ready.

But Gotch Ear couldn't break Sam's hold on his throat. He'd lost his knife in the scramble, and he couldn't pull Sam loose with his bare hands. Sam had gotten the grip he wanted when he first tied into Gotch Ear; and from there on, all he had to do was just hold what he had.

He was still lying there in the water with his eyes squeezed shut, hanging grimly to his throat hold on a dead Apache when Herb Haley finally got around to ramming the butt end of his quirt between the clamped jaws and prizing them apart.

This came later, though, and I never saw it. I didn't even get to see Sam finish off Gotch Ear, because a sudden wild whoop and Lisbeth's shrill scream reached out to me from across the valley, jolting my attention away from Sam's battle.

I saw an Apache springing up out of the tall grass to land astride the scare-running horse Lisbeth rode.

It was Broken Nose—you could bet on that. And you could bet it was a calculated thing, his picking Lisbeth's horse, when he could just as easily have mounted another and got away faster.

Lisbeth was his captive and he meant to keep her.

It didn't seem possible for Broken Nose to have crawled all that far since I'd glanced a ball off his shield and Sanderson's shots had sent him plunging for cover in the grass. But there he went, making off with Lisbeth, riding straight away from me, already so far up the opposite slope that it would stretch a gun barrel to reach him—and me with an empty rifle!

I was shaken, but I didn't panic this time. I reloaded fast, paying no attention to the shouts of the men with Papa or to the crashing reports of Sanderson's rifle.

Sanderson might be missing; but more likely, his lead was falling short. I kept this in mind when at last I drew a bead on the fleeing figures, now made so small by distance that the thin front sight of my rifle all but hid them.

What I wanted to do was kill the horse; but, shooting at that range, there was always a chance that I'd kill Lisbeth. Thought of this brought the ache of fear high in my throat. But I had no choice; I drew a coarse bead and held steady and squeezed off my shot, then watched my rifle ball clip grass stalks fifty yards behind the running horse.

I was too heartsick to reload. What was the use? My rifle wouldn't carry that far. I was closer than anybody, yet even I couldn't reach them.

From down in the wash, I heard Wiley Crup's voice, lifted high in desperate protest.

"But I might hit the girl!"

Searcy's blustery shout lifted even higher. "Tech a hair on that girl, and I'll blow a two-foot gap on yore backbone!"

I looked in that direction. I saw Wiley Crup, down off his horse, with the long barrel of his rifle laid across his saddle. He took aim. I heard the mighty blast of the Big

Fifty and saw Wiley stagger back from its recoil in a cloud of gunsmoke.

I started up and looked ahead in time to see Broken Nose knocked ten feet sideways off that running horse.

He nearly took Lisbeth with him, but she managed to hang on a few seconds longer before she flung herself free and disappeared into the grass.

She was up almost instantly and running back down the slope toward us, scared out of her wits, I guess; but I was no longer scared for her. I'd seen the spread-eagled body of Broken Nose go flying through the air; and even at that distance, I could tell that it was limp as a wet dishrag before it ever hit the ground. Broken Nose wasn't going to molest Lisbeth again, or anybody else.

Herb Haley's voice rose high-pitched from down in the draw. "Man alive, what a shot!" he marveled. "A thousand yards, if it's a foot!"

But Wiley's shot wasn't enough to satisfy Uncle Pack. He shouted at the men, furious with impatience.

"All right!" he stormed. "Wiley's made a brag shot. But that ain't killin' them what's down in the grass. Spread out and git after 'em. Now! Before they git away!"

His anger lashed Haley and Crup into action. They mounted and rode out, combing the grass for hidden Indians.

But Papa and Searcy paid Uncle Pack no mind. Papa rode off to meet Lisbeth, while Searcy heaved himself out of the saddle and sprawled in the grass.

I reloaded, but didn't wait around to see if anybody flushed an Indian. All I wanted now was to get my hands on Little Arliss and Savage Sam, to hug them up close and feel the warm life in them, to be on hand and see the look in Lisbeth's eyes when Papa brought her in.

I didn't think that look would make me feel awkward and shy any more. I thought that, now, I could meet it head on and feel proud of what I saw there.

I struck a buffalo trail that skirted the foot of the hill. It didn't lead straight to where I was going; but it led pretty close and made for easier walking. I followed it, listening to, but not really hearing, the Indian hunters calling to each other across the valley.

I shuffled along in a daze. I'd suffered too much body pain. I'd clung too long to the ragged edge of despair. And, now that it was all over, I felt too numb with relief to take any real notice of anything any more.

At least, that's the way I seemed to feel, up until I came even with Arliss and old man Searcy and left the trail to go to them.

I hadn't taken more than four or five steps out into the grass when I jerked up short, all my senses screaming danger.

It was the Comanche!

He'd played it smart. He'd crawled within fifty steps of Little Arliss and Bud Searcy, knowing that was the place we were least likely to look for him.

Now, he lay in the grass, staring straight up at me.

I guess it was surprise that held me at first. For a second, I couldn't seem to think what to do. Then it must have been the look in the Comanche's eyes that kept me stood off.

There was no fear in those black eyes, and no hate—just that same intense curiosity with which he'd studied me and Lisbeth and Little Arliss from the first. Best I could tell, he was just lying there with a bloody hole through his left side, waiting to see what I would do.

Wiley Crup's voice came to me from across the valley. "Here's a dead one!"

"Hang the dead ones, you fool!" Uncle Pack shouted back at him. "It's the live ones we're after! 'Fore they git away!"

Well, here lay a live one. Right at my feet. All I had to do to keep him from getting away was to shoot him.

Then why didn't I go ahead and do it?

To this day, I don't have a real satisfying answer.

During the thick of the fight, I'd wanted to kill him, I'd tried hard to kill him, and if I had, I'd have been proud of it afterward.

But now, with the fight all over and done, with Lisbeth and Little Arliss safe once more—well, somehow, things were different.

I could no longer look on him as a threat. All I could see was a badly wounded man, lying helpless, without one weapon left to defend himself. He lay there, looking death square in the face without flinching, without even appearing much concerned about it. In fact, the feeling I got was that what he wanted most of all was to bridge the wide gap that lay between his way of thinking and mine.

I left him there and went on down to where Little Arliss was squatted over Savage Sam, petting and praising him and talking up a storm with old man Searcy.

I went, fighting back the tears and hoping desperately that the Comanche got away.

But I still can't tell you why.

Sam

BEN TODD and Lester White rode in and helped to round up the scattered horses. Night as close on us; but tired and shaken up as we all were, nderson ordered fresh horses to be caught and saddled.

"The way I see it," he said, "we'll be smart to make de-apart tracks away from here."

The only ones to argue with Sanderson about moving on re Uncle Pack and Bud Searcy.

"I can't go on," Searcy whimpered. "I'm a dyin' man, nderson. All's left for me now is the cold grave and the isty Beyond."

He lay with his head in Lisbeth's lap, weeping with self- y while Lisbeth bathed his face and cried and begged n not to die.

Sanderson looked down on the old man for a moment, dying, then spoke. "Well, to tell the truth, Mr. Searcy," said, "we can't hardly spare the time to dig you that ave right now. Not with every redskin in hearing of our nfire done drifting this way, hoping to lift some extra ir. You'd be doing us a big favor to hold off dying for a ell. Till we can get further away from this slaughter und."

If Searcy suspected he was getting hoorawed, he didn't ue the point.

Uncle Pack, though, was harder to convince. He wept, , with the rage and bitterness of defeat.

"But I tell you," he stormed, "we've let three of them stiles git away."

"We got the children," Sanderson said. "That's what we ne for."

145

"What I come for is to kill Injuns," Uncle Pack sai
fiercely. "Right down to their last louse and nit! We let a⯑
one git away, I've broke a sworn promise to my dea⯑
woman and childer!"

Sanderson said bluntly, "Uncle Pack, your woman a⯑
children, they're gone. We're all sorry about it. But ⯑
don't aim to risk the lives of more children on account ⯑
it!"

He left Uncle Pack to study on that while he went out
where Wiley Crup was saddling a horse.

"Wiley," I heard him say, "there ain't another man ⯑
Texas could have made the shot you made, and I wa⯑
you to know we all appreciate it."

As much as I hated feeling beholden to a man like Wil⯑
Crup, I had to admit that Sanderson was right.

But Wiley didn't warm to Sanderson's praise. He glanc⯑
to where old man Searcy lay, grunting and groaning, e⯑
joying his misery.

"That flannel-mouth old fool!" he sneered. "A hair-⯑
miscalculation, and I'd a-kilt that little girl."

"The thing is," Sanderson said, "you didn't make th⯑
miscalculation."

We mounted and rode east up the long slope of ⯑
valley, driving the loose horses. Papa and Herb Haley ro⯑
on either side of Bud Searcy, keeping him propped up ⯑
the saddle. Lisbeth rode close by, silent and worried. I h⯑
the grunting Sam across my lap and listened to Little Arli⯑
talking like a house afire. Most of his talk was directed ⯑
Lester White.

"You see us?" he demanded of White. "Me 'n' old Sa⯑
We done him under, didn't we? Cleaned that Injun's plo⯑
for him. Learnt him a lesson about killin' old Jumper. W⯑
a-wiped up plenty others, too, if they'd a-come arou⯑
messin' with us. Me 'n' old Sam, we ain't to be tampe⯑
with!"

All the excitement had Arliss wound up tighter than ⯑
eight-day clock. You never heard such brag talk ⯑
whopping big lies as he went on to tell. And White, he ⯑
tened and kept a sober face and nodded his head ev⯑
now and then, letting on that he believed every word o⯑

We rode till long after moonrise, till Little Arliss ran

f wild talk, till I dozed in the saddle and old man Searcy
ad long since given up complaining.

Sometime past midnight, we came to a little creek where
here was wood and water and shallow caves in the rock
anks to hide the light of a campfire from any prowling
ndians.

Here, we unsaddled and pitched camp. Sanderson put
uards out. The rest of us cooked and ate and slept till
round noontime the next day, then changed guards and
te and slept some more.

It seemed like I couldn't get enough of either one, sleep
r food. Half the time, while I ate, I was more asleep than
wake, so that my recollections of what happened there are
retty fuzzy.

I do remember that somebody shot a yearling buffalo
nd how good the hump ribs tasted after Ben Todd gave
hem a slow roasting over a mesquite-wood fire. I remem-
er, too, what a bad case of the walking fidgets Papa had.

"She'll be near about crazy with worry," I heard him tell
anderson, and knew that he was talking about Mama, and
new that he was right.

But Sanderson only shook his head. "I know, Jim," he
aid. "But we can't afford to travel by day. Injuns can spot
s too easy. And we nearly got to feed and rest up these
ttle old younguns and old man Searcy. They're all worn
o a frazzle."

So we kept eating and sleeping till dark came on, then
addled and moved out.

We traveled with Sanderson riding nearly a mile in the
ead and Uncle Pack about that far behind and with
ankers out on either side. We rode all that night, ate and
ept all the next day, then pulled out again about dark.

Like before, we were traveling too far and too fast. We
ever got enough rest or enough to eat, and hanging over
s every minute was the threat of running into an Indian
ar party too big for us to handle. Twice, Sanderson
otted the glow of campfires far out on the dark prairie
nd rode back to lead us around them.

In spite of all this, I could still feel myself mending. Most
the pain was gone from my wounds, and my sunburned
in began healing and peeling till I looked as shaggy as a

rusty tree lizard at shedding time. Every day, it seemed like I felt stronger.

What gave us the worst trouble was old man Searcy. Night and day, in and out of the saddle, he kept dying and dying. We sure got worn out with his eternal complaining.

The thing that riled me so was the way, at every camp, he kept calling on Lisbeth to fetch him water and food, to pull his boots off, to wash his feet, to grease his sunburn— keeping her in a trot every minute of our resting time, like maybe she hadn't suffered through everything he had, and plenty more. I finally got so fed up that I jumped Lisbeth out about it.

It was at a water hole somewhere in the Big Spring country. I was cutting mesquite thorns for Lisbeth to use to pin together her torn dress. Old man Searcy started calling in that quavery, pore-mouth voice.

"Lisbeth, honey. Would you kindly fetch yore pore ol' grandpa a drink of water?"

Lisbeth started to go to him. It made me mad. I grabbed her arm and held her.

"Let him fetch his own water, for a change!" I said.

Lisbeth looked at me in surprise. "But, Travis," she said, "he's too old and worn out. He's nearly dead!"

"Nearly dead, my hind foot," I said. "That's just put-on and always has been."

Lisbeth looked away, staring out across the grass. Finally, she said, "Even if you're right, it still wouldn't make any difference."

"How come?" I demanded. "You mean you like being run ragged by that old windbag?"

That cut deeper than I'd meant it to. It brought the start of tears to her eyes.

"Travis, you know I'm all Grandpa's got," she said. "He's been good to me. And menfolks—well, it seems like they're never real happy without they got some woman at their beck and call."

Back of me, I heard a short laugh. I wheeled around. It was Burn Sanderson and Ben Todd. I hadn't heard them come up, but there they stood, both wearing wide, knowing grins.

Sanderson pulled a sober look and spoke to Ben like me and Lisbeth weren't there.

"You know, Ben," he said, "that Travis Coates is a smart boy. He's done found him a girl with more understanding of a man's needs than most women ever get round to learning."

I felt a blush spread both ways from my neck. I liked Sanderson; but right now, I could have clubbed him over the head.

In a way, Sam was as much trouble as old man Searcy. After his long chase, he was so sore-footed and stiff in the joints he couldn't hardly stand without whimpering. He suffered so much that every scrap of food and every drop of water had to be packed to him; and when it came time to leave, there was no question about his needing to ride.

The trouble was, he seemed to get worse instead of better. I got real worried about him.

But Papa didn't. "That old dog's just pulling the wool over your eyes," he told me one night. "He's sore-footed, all right, but he's not all that beat-up."

"Why would he want to do that?" I demanded.

"On account of he's got a taste of high living and don't aim to give it up," Papa said. "You keep pampering him, and you'll have him so rotten spoilt, he won't be worth knocking in the head."

That got my fur up. "What of it?" I demanded. "He's earned the right to some spoiling. Hadn't been for him, we'd never on earth have saved Lisbeth and Little Arliss, and you know it!"

But when I started to lift Sam into the saddle, Papa put his foot down.

"Leave him lay," he ordered. "He just as well learn now he's not going to ride horseback for the rest of his life!"

So, with me and Little Arliss both hurt and mad about it, we rode off and left Sam lying where he was.

The minute he saw that we weren't going to pack him, Sam rolled over and lay flat on his back, holding four limp feet in the air to show how crippled he was. And the farther off we rode, the louder and more pitiful his howling got.

Finally, Arliss couldn't stand it any longer. He burst in tears and wheeled his horse around.

"I ain't a-going off and leaving old Sam!" he stormed.

And back toward Sam he went at a gallop, paying mind to Papa's threat of taking a quirt to him.

Well, the danger of Indians was too great. We couldn let Arliss leave the bunch. All we could do was go back f him.

We found him down off his horse, hugging the whimpe ing Sam and telling him not to worry, that he wasn't goi off and leave him, ever.

Papa was about ready to make good his threat with quirt when Lester White stepped down and lifted Sam his arms.

"Mr. Coates," he said, "I'd consider it an honor to sha my saddle with this Genuine Amalgamated Pot-Hound f as long as he cares to ride."

He grinned at Papa, showing that he'd caught on Papa's and Sanderson's spoofing.

So Papa gave up there, and Sam rode till the morni when we finally reached home.

It was just before daybreak when we arrived, but Man already had a candle lit; and I don't guess I'll ever ta more comfort from anything than I did from the sight our little old two-room cabin, squatted there on the slo of the hill, with warm yellow candlelight streaming throu the porthole windows.

We'd been gone less than ten days, but it seemed like year, and there'd been plenty of times when I'd never e pected to see that cabin again.

Papa hollered, "Hello, the house!" and the door open a crack and a gun barrel was poked through.

Tom McDougal called out, "Who is it?"

But Mama had done recognized Papa's voice. She flu the door wide open and came flying out, calling, "Ji Jim!" and all but dragged Papa out of the saddle before could dismount.

McDougal and his woman, Sarah, they came out, to and stood in the candlelight, smiling and looking please while Mama laughed and cried at the same time and we

rom one to the other, hugging and kissing everybody, even
o Wiley Crup, who was so startled that he dropped his Big
ifty and got sand in the barrel.

It was about then that from out near the corncrib, we
heard a loud cackling, then the frantic squawkings of a
caught hen.

"It's that confounded bobcat again!" Tom McDougal
complained. He started on a run toward the chicken roost,
calling for somebody to bring him a light.

Before he had time to get halfway there, we heard the
angry squawl of the cat, then the snarling roar of Savage
Sam.

Sam and the cat mixed it hot and heavy for a minute,
and we'd all started running toward the fight when Sam let
out a shrill yelp that told us the cat had got in a mighty
painful lick.

After that, everything but the cackling chickens was quiet
or about half a minute while we ran on toward the roost.
Then, a hundred yards off, we heard Sam open, his trail
voice ringing out loud and urgent.

The way he was driving on the trail of the bobcat, you'd
have thought he had never heard tell of a sore foot.

And sure enough, right close behind him, we heard
Little Arliss yell.

"That's a-taking him yonder, Sam! Go git him, boy!"

Mama screamed at Arliss to come back and Papa threatened him with a whipping, but I knew better than to waste
my breath. I wheeled and lit out for the saddled horses still
standing at the front-yard gate. I mounted the big rawboned bay I'd ridden so far and quirted him into a run.

When finally I caught up with Arliss, I handled him just
like the dead Gotch Ear would have done. I reached down
and grabbed me a fistful of his tousled hair. I yanked him
up across my saddle and held him there, kicking and yelling and threatening me with murder.

"You turn me a-loose, Travis Coates," he screamed.
"You don't turn me a-loose, I'll bust you with a rock!"

He didn't have a rock, so I paid no mind to his threats.
headed back for the cabin, holding a tight grip on the
back of his neck.

I aimed to make sure I got there without losing an ear.

## About the Author

Fred Gipson was born in 1908 in Mason, Texas, where he now lives. He grew up on a dry-land farm and has worked at everything from cotton-picking to driving a caterpillar tractor. After attending the University of Texas, he worked as a reporter for various Texas newspapers and for a few months was a feature writer for the Denver *Post* Sunday magazine section. He took up free-lance writing in 1940, the same year he was married, and has published a great number of articles and short stories, which have appeared in *Collier's, Holiday, Reader's Digest,* and *South-west Review,* to name a few.

Mr. Gipson's first book, FABULOUS EMPIRE, was published in 1946 by Houghton Mifflin. In 1949 he came to Harper's with his novel HOUND DOG MAN, which was a Book-of-the-Month Club selection. Since then Harper's has published most of Mr. Gipson's work, which has included books for both adults and for children. Among these are THE HOME PLACE, THE TRAIL DRIVING ROOSTER and OLD YELLER. OLD YELLER won the 1959 William Allen White Award, First Sequoyah Book Award (Oklahoma) 1959, Pacific Northwest Library Association Award, 1959 and was a best seller.

Mr. Gipson now lives with his wife and two sons on a part of the old Gipson homestead, where he devotes his time to writing and to managing a small stock farm. He raises cattle and hogs, and in season hunts deer, wild turkey and quail. He prefers fly fishing to all other outdoor sports and is interested in the study of soil and plant growth. He has been conducting a number of experiments in the re-seeding of rangeland to native and imported grasses.